Praise for RISEN

I loved Elizabeth Watasin's graphic novel, Charm School. *Now, after too long an absence, she has returned to print with fiction.* RISEN *is only the first of what promises to be a thoroughly enjoyable (if delightfully disturbing) series. Roll over, Arthur Conan Doyle! Move over, Philip Pullman!*

- Trina Robbins
Writer, Herstorian, author of The Chicagoland detective Agency series and *Lily Renee, Escape Artist*

RISEN *is as interesting for the things half-seen as the things shown clearly: the elegant exotica of steampunk London, the mysterious natures of both the not-dead protagonists, the elements unexpected even in steampunk, such as the 'artificial' ghost's faith and ethics. I am well and truly drawn in, and am eager for more.*

- Carla Speed McNeil, creator of *FINDER*

Books by Elizabeth Watasin

The Dark Victorian: BONES

Sundark: An Elle Black Penny Dread

Charm School Graphique, Vol 1-5

Charm School Digital, No 1-10

This BOOK belongs to:

Credits:

Cover Art by Phatpuppy Creations
phatpuppyart.com
Cover design and art by Elizabeth Watasin

Cover model is Elizabeth Worth
www.modelmayhem.com/3122503
Custom Wardrobe Creation: Cavalyn Galano
www.facebook.com/CavalynDesign
Makeup/Hair: Nadya Rutman
www.bynadya.com
Photography: Teresa Yeh Photography
www.teresayeh.com

Typography by Tom Orzechowski and Lois Buhalis
www.serifsup.com

Interior Illustrations by Elizabeth Watasin

Editing by JoSelle Vanderhooft
www.joselle-vanderhooft.com

Acknowledgements

Thanks to Jody Susskind for critique, commiseration, and encouragement.

The Dark Victorian: RISEN

Volume 1

By
Elizabeth Watasin

A-GIRL STUDIO

An A-Girl Studio book
published 2012 in the USA.

For additional information, please contact:
A-Girl Studio
P.O. Box 213, Burbank, CA 91503 U.S.A.
www.a-girlstudio.com

ISBN: 978-1-936622-01-6
Library of Congress Control Number: 2012919475
First paperback edition, 2012

❀

To
All
The Women
Who Brought Us
Here
in 100 Years.

Our eyes are
clear.

CHAPTER ONE

"I Am Here."

In the dead of night, in the darkest part of London, gaslights still burned inside an East End penny gaff. A large, slow man in worn cap and coat shuffled out. He held a covered bird cage by the handle. Raucous laughter burst behind him, followed by hard thumps on tables to the beat of a fast sprightly tune. He pushed through the costermen in work clothes drinking gin from mugs and smoking pipes near the light of the entrance. Women slowly walked on the bulging, cracked cobbled street that swelled from the gases trapped beneath. Lit only by dim small windows, the women drifted in and out of the mist that escaped leaky steam pipes.

"Show us yer birdy," a woman called invitingly from the darkness, but the man with the cage ignored her. Far above, a train rumbled past on elevated tracks and disappeared into the yellow smoke rising from the gas works. He saw its bright windows flash. Its destination was the same as his.

He shuffled down dark, narrow, winding streets which eventually widened and became gas lit, the decrepit tenements left behind for closed shops and darkened boarding houses. He reached the thoroughfare where coffee houses glowed and the thick cut glass windows of taverns flickered. Hansom cabs and their horses trotted past, still transporting fares. Two horses and a brougham waited before a private club's secured entryway. The metal iris entrance opened in a spiral, spilling bright light. The music of a dance could be heard, and a white-whiskered army captain accompanied by a gaily dressed young woman stepped over the circle entrance and emerged.

The man with the bird cage turned at the end of the street. The sounds of dancing and merriment abruptly cut once the iris door spun shut, and the horses and brougham started, overtaking the man and passing him. He continued, shuffling by the windows of the newspaper publishers. Men waited by their delivery carts and barrows while loitering newsboys jostled. More boys, blackened from the printing presses, smoked. Their animated talk faded from the man's ears just as the light of the newspaper offices gave way to shadows.

A light drizzle was falling when he arrived at the wide street lined by the still courts of law. A black building stretched to the night sky. Huge metal power ducts ran from the earth into its sides. A train several stories above whistled its arrival and rumbled into the building. There, night clerks and workers who lived outside the city would disembark, enter the building's steam powered moving platforms, and travel to street level where they would hurry to their night time positions. If the man could read, the chiseled words above the entrance would have said:

TSC, PRINCE ALBERT'S OWN, 1875, *Malum quidem nullum esse sine aliquo bono.* —There is, to be sure, no evil without something good.

The massive entry doors were ajar. The man entered.

In the gas lit lobby lined with closed shops, one kiosk was available for business: the lending library and newspaper stand of W. H. Smith and Sons. The news agent sat within, reading by lobby light and surrounded by the fresh penny rags and periodicals he sold. Metal tubes with doors ran from the lobby floor to the ceiling. They held small, ascending chambers. Several doors immediately hissed open, steam escaping. Workmen and ruddy-faced women in their shawls emerged and walked for the building entrance.

The man shuffled through the crowd for the doors of the last ascension tube. They were solid black. He searched the dirty kerchief tied around his neck and fished out a crumpled black ribbon trimmed in silver. Attached was a shield-shaped, engraved jet pin. The engraving was of a silver crown and sword with wings. He held the pin against the shield-shaped recess in the black door and watched it sizzle. A puff of smoke rose. The black doors slid open and the man returned the pin, cool to the touch, to his neck kerchief.

He entered the ascending room, the platform decompressing under his weight. A stick lever was positioned to the far left of a brass half dial marked in numbered increments. He pulled the lever all the way to the right and held tight to the railing. The platform hissed, steam rising in plumes. The room rose rapidly, shooting the man from the ground floor to the topmost story of the Secret Commission Building.

When the doors opened, a vast laboratory floor lay before him. It was quiet except for the gentle, rhythmic click and whistle from the large machines sprouting out of the floor and winding into the ceiling. Metal panels hid the skylights. Wood platforms divided the work area vertically; some led to doors or held locked cabinets full of thick books, others stored obscure and precious objects. There were tables laden with chemistry equipment and other wire and tube set-ups for experiments. Wooden stairs led down from the various suspended platforms to the main floor.

Seated at a table high above worked an old man in shirtsleeves and a leather apron. His bald pate was wreathed with wild white hair. The thick spectacles he wore clicked and rotated their multiple lenses as he carefully dropped liquid on a glowing mineral in a bowl. His notebooks were propped open before him. He spun in his chair at hearing the plodding shuffle of the man with the bird cage and looked down.

"Ah!" Dr. Gatly Fall said, rubbing his hands. His mouth widened in an open mouth grin, revealing cavernous black. "Set him on the table, Mud."

Mud set the cage down and pulled the cover off. Inside was a man's bony bleached skull wearing a black top hat. His name was Jim Dastard.

"Well you have me, by hell! What is it now?" Jim said. In fury he rattled.

"Welcome, Mr. Dastard! Always a pleasure!" Fall said. "It was necessary to fetch you. And safely. Didn't want Mud to drop you."

"Bastard," Jim said as Mud slowly twisted the cage apart. "Next flood or rainstorm I'll melt your Golem."

Mud picked Jim up and set him upon the table. Jim, with great effort, tipped himself back so his eye sockets could see Fall.

"Oh tut, Mr. Dastard, forgive the lump. I've good news! Your leave is officially over. You're getting a new partner."

"Billy's only been dead three days. You'll not bring him back?"

"Oh he, well, as you've reported, oh." Fall heavily sighed. "Yes, he wasn't of very strong psychic mettle, was he? Foolish, uneducated. . . slow. The Commission decided he should be laid to permanent rest."

"The boy had a good heart, though meeting a train head-on never impressed a train. You were the one who gave him his second death! He should have never been resurrected and judged an agent in the first place!"

"I can only work with what I get from the gallows," Fall protested, his mouth widening.

"What you get is any poor executed soul the Commission decides is not worth damning and sending along to hell just yet," Jim said. "And sometimes they decide wrong!"

"Oh yes. And such fun that is. But oh! These past months I've been working on a prize, a real prize. I must say, even His Highness reviewed my latest work and gave his royal endorsement."

"A nice shot in the arm," Jim said sarcastically.

Dr. Fall's mouth worked as he peered in confusion down at Jim. He fumbled for a notebook, opened it, and began writing. Jim rattled on the table.

"Why you—stop that!" he cried. "Stop that at once! I've told you before you're not allowed to write down whatever I say!"

"Oh, but it's just so queer, Dastard," Fall laughed. "The things that fall out of your teeth. Queer as Egyptian pyramids."

"Go sit on one," Jim said. "I was informed of my next case then kidnapped and brought here. Shall we get on with it?"

"Yes," Fall said. He moved for a bell and rang it. "My best resurrection yet." He swiveled in his chair to face the door behind him. "An artificial ghost."

"A ghost?" Jim said.

Beyond the door, deliberate and purposeful steps echoed. There was the accompanying tap of a stick. Jim listened and wondered at the validity of so solid a 'ghost' when the door opened.

An extraordinarily pale and statuesque woman stepped forward, her high-collared fitted dress sweeping the floor. A cravat pinned by a cameo skull brooch adorned her throat. A silver-handled ironwood walking stick was in her gloved hand. Her body held a subtle, spectral aura. The shimmer of it bleached the color from her clothing and hat.

"Jim Dastard," Fall said. "Meet Artifice."

Jim had never seen such stature on a woman. The average bobby was five foot ten inches, but he was certain even

without the hat she was a good four inches their superior. She
was broad of shoulder, small of waist, and with a generous chest
so well-fitted by her bodice Jim felt she might deflect bullets.
She addressed him, her voice solemn yet gentle.

"Friend," she said.

Jim's jaw dropped.

"She's QUAKER!" he shouted.

"Ha!" Fall shouted back. "HA!"

"What, you didn't think I would know?!" Jim said. "Friends
of the Truth? Children of the Light? She may not dress like
one, but there's no mistaking what she just said!"

"Sharp, Mr. Dastard. Sharp. Yes, she is Quaker."

"Why?!" Jim cried. "They are pacifist, charitable, and boring! How can a humble porridge-eater confront the horrors we
fight?"

"Don't forget virtuous, which you did request for your next
partner since your last one was so, oh, wayward."

"A soused herring was what Billy Black was! And now you
give me Lady Temperance?"

"Artifice," Fall said, his eyes widening in mirth. "Was 'designed to order.' She was and is Quaker. But her abilities will
surprise you. Very much."

The walking stick tapped. Artifice descended from Fall's
platform. Jim watched her take each step with calm awareness.
Her eyes upon him were kind.

"A queenly Clydesdale," Jim said miserably.

Doors opened across the room, and Artifice turned her head.
Jim hopped to see. A tall, thin man with a lean face and thick
moustache entered followed by a clerk. He quickly descended
the steps and joined Artifice on the floor.

"Director," Jim and Fall addressed him in unison.

"Gentlemen," the director said. He turned to Artifice. "Well,
Artifice. It's time to fulfill your duty to the Crown. Upon
your execution it was decided you'd be resurrected into a form

and purpose best suited as an agent of His Highness, Prince Albert's Secret Commission, and that you would dedicate your life, as it has been given back to you, to the service you will now bear; ridding England of its supernatural evils. Raise your right hand."

Artifice switched her walking stick to her left and did so.

"Do you swear to champion the good and true, to fight foremost and first the dark that threatens England, to shield our helpless, to uphold the light and banish evil, to bear this sacred trust with sacrifice even unto death, in fealty and loyalty to God and Crown?"

There was a long silence in which the director and Artifice stared at each other.

"Swear to this oath under God and Crown."

"Erm hrm! Quaker," Jim mumbled.

"Make your solemn affirmation to God and the Crown," the Director said.

"I give my solemn affirmation to God," Artifice said.

The director lowered his hand. "Your loyalty is accepted." He turned to the clerk who opened a small black box and handed it to him. The director retrieved the black and silver badge with its black ribbon and pinned it to Artifice's chest. "Wear this as your symbol of truth and duty. Congratulations." He surveyed the other men in the room. "Gentlemen."

"Sir!" Jim said. The director departed with his clerk. Once the doors shut behind him, Jim laughed.

"Church of England; he should have remembered that you wouldn't take a Protestant oath. Well! Let's get out of here," Jim said to Artifice. When she approached he wanted to gulp. She was an imposing figure for a woman. She gently picked him up and straightened his top hat. Suddenly Jim felt at ease. As Artifice made her way around the laboratory for the ascending room doors, Jim called back to the doctor.

"Fall, as always, never a pleasure."

Once the doors closed his new partner studied the lever control.

"Set that thing at "4." I don't want to arrive at ground yet," Jim said. Artifice did so, and the platform hissed. It sank and they descended the building.

"Hmph," Jim said as Artifice looked about the moving room in fascination. "'Designed to order.' I've never heard Fall say that of an agent before. Someone requested you should be thus, retaining your Quaker nature, but for the life of me I can't understand why. You're already butting heads with the official religion. And why so tall? Fall can manipulate many things in a resurrection, but physical height is a new one to me."

"Friend," Artifice said. "I only know myself as I am. As way opens, thee shall help me discover."

"I just did. No 'thou,' young Quaker? Thee is a 'thee'er,' then?"

"Friend?"

Their platform slowed to a stop, and Artifice briefly adjusted to the lack of propulsion.

"Just tell me what first comes to your head—in answer to my question."

She paused in thought.

"To use those words which confer title and flattery is unlike the Friends," she finally said. "'Thou' is also 'you,' an address of class. By my address of 'thee' is our equality assured."

"Some of your brethren still use 'thou.'"

"I have shared my belief," Artifice said firmly.

"Ha ha! Such resolve! A very young Quaker, indeed. When did you first awake?"

"Two days ago, I believe."

"As blank as a block of marble. Well, at least I got my teeth into you before they could put all sorts of notions into your head. Let me look at you. I shall read thy physiognomy."

Artifice held Jim up in her hands so his eye sockets could

gaze directly. She had strong bone structure for her sex; defined cheekbones, a well sloped nose, and a firm broad jaw. Her mouth had a gentle quirk to one corner, one that could denote mirth or grimness. She wasn't pretty by the usual standards of feminine beauty, but her features held strength and honesty, which Jim suspected could inspire fraternity. Her skin's unnatural paleness reached her eyes, divesting them of discernable colour though the light of intelligence showed clear. Her patient gaze held humour. Dastard was not a practitioner in physiognomy—the configuration and interpretation of people's features. He did read much in eyes however, even when they lied.

"Clear as a Quaker," he said.

"What dost thee see?"

"That you'll not last the day. Well, to it, then! Let's get this bucket moving!"

She pulled the lever for the ground floor. When the doors opened, the lobby was lively. People hurried back and forth to the ascension tube doors. As Artifice walked through the crowd with Jim in her hand, passers-by started and gave her a wide berth. She held Jim up before her like a serving tray. With his eye sockets forward, he led her approach and could guide her if he wished. She passed the book kiosk where a delivery man was setting down stacks of periodicals and papers. While he and the seller worked, she turned her head and saw a woman standing there.

She was a young lady in her mid-twenties, dark haired with arched brows and a rosy tint to her lips and cheek. Her hair was disorderly beneath her hat. One side of her face wore a fitted leather mask. Her eyes were blue, and at the sight of Artifice her lips parted and her eyes grew wide with a strange, deep delight and profound awe. Artifice returned the gaze and then had to break it; the intensity unsettled her.

Artifice moved for the wide open doors of the Secret Commission and stepped outside for the first time.

The sky's foggy dark was edged with glowing light, signaling sunrise. Artifice stood on the sidewalk and scanned the street with its hurrying carts and cabs, barrows and pedestrians, all aiming for respective destinations. The air was thunderous with the sound of wheels and hooves. She chose a direction and began to walk, looking at the faces of men and women, young girls and children—a bootblack at a corner was swiftly shining a shoe, and little street sweepers were industriously clearing a gentleman's path. Clerks were streaming to the courthouses. The buildings and walls around her were covered in advertisements in huge bold letters, hawking chocolate, pills, shows, and legal services. She smelled the dung, animals, and people. Carts carrying bundled newspapers trundled past. Boys of every size ran with freshly printed paper beneath their arms and disappeared between buildings.

"Fleet Street," she said, seeing the newspaper offices.

"Memory surgery," Jim said in her hand. "Amazing trick. You'll remember nothing of yourself, your previous life, your identity; none of it. But you'll know how to dress yourself, how to speak, what meat pies are and what they taste like; butter, treacle, pudding, ginger beer, who the Queen of England, Punch and Judy, and Father Christmas are, and your letters and numbers if you were suitably educated. Let's buy a paper. That boy there, he has the one we want. You'll recall your coinage as well and count accordingly."

She did, retrieving the pence from the allowance the Commission had issued to her. The boy bravely thrust the paper into her hand once he had the money and ran away. Jim next requested that she buy some cigarettes from a tobacconist just then pulling his blinds open for business. Another purchase from the frightened proprietor, and they were soon seated in a coffee shop, Jim puffing on the cigarette Artifice helpfully lit for him. The smoke emerged from his eye sockets.

"That's better," he sighed. "Didn't get to rest at all once I was summoned to pick you up. Fire and smoke is what fuels me. A few matches make a good snack and a candle can suffice, but a nice stove fire sufficiently invigorates. Billy, God bless that dimwit, was a voracious coal eater."

'*Dimwit*,' Artifice thought, not recognizing the word.

" What about you? Discovered what sates you? Porridge, perhaps? Oats? Hay?"

"I've no hunger," Artifice said. "And if I'm to be a Clydesdale, 'twill be will be."

"Oh 'twill! Say, you look like you've trouble with your chair."

"'Tis not the chair." She shifted. "I've a metal bustle." She said it with mild distaste. The object in question gave a metallic creak in response.

Jim chuckled around his cigarette. "Your second clue. You were not previously born well-to-do. Though you carry that lovely dress better than a blue blood. Sit forward, I believe that's how the ladies handle it. Now, my young Friend. We've a case, you and I, and just so I can enjoy my breakfast of smoke and ash, I'll let the newspaper explain it. Find the article by Helia Skycourt. She's a good journalist, that; supernatural events are her specialty, and what we're after is of a very dark sort. You look like you can read. Can you do it aloud?"

"I can and shall," Artifice murmured. She placed her walking stick upon her arm. The curved silver handle's head was of a deer; the other end came to the blunt point of a horn. She opened the paper and began reading to Jim.

"The *Times*

"Tuesday, 9 March, of this year 1880

"Who Is The Rogue Re-animationist?

"Helia Skycourt

"Death has struck again, and his vengeful instruments are the bodies of those that should be dead. Recall that on Sunday, 7 March, one Culver Drury, a cat meat seller, was skinning his wares near Whitechapel Market when the carcasses reanimated and attacked him, biting him so severely he died within the hour. On Monday, 8 March, in the traffic of Houndsditch a cab man's horse collapsed. Aware that it had perished, Horatio Bottoms descended in anger to whip the carcass when it rose again, bit him by the throat, and flung him about until dead. It then kicked the cab to pieces, severely injuring the passengers. Witnesses who escaped its fury report that the beast was unquestionably dead, having broken its neck upon its first expiration. In both instances the resurrected animals were put to second and final rest by the courageous and swift response of our local policemen.

"Who is raising these dead? Only by royal sanction of His Royal Highness and Her Majesty is one man allowed in all of the British Empire to practice resurrection, and that is in the service of Prince Albert's Secret Commission. By the power vested in this personage are condemned souls given back to the service of England, formidable, intelligent, and effective in their duty to protect. The reanimations of these animal corpses respond with a savagery that gives evidence; the spirit of such animals had fled, and this reckless re-animationist has summoned to his bidding and to dark action, their bodies for violent recourse."

⤚ ⤙

"Art, could you light me another, please?" Jim interrupted. "And order a coffee to give to the beggar woman there; since we're keeping these seats warm we should pay the house tithe."

Artifice put the paper down and in distraction did as Jim asked. The beggar woman huddled at her seat refused the coffee from the server girl and spat at them.

"Devil'rs!" she said.

"Art, did you finish reading?" Jim asked   while Artifice observed the beggar woman in surprise. She picked up the paper and resumed reading aloud.

". . .This rogue black arts practitioner may not be content with re-animating the bodies of animals. Around 8 the evening of Mr. Bottoms's death, another victim of murder has been found, John "Honest" Harvey, a Ragged School teacher dedicated to helping poor boys, though the complaints of certain parents have been duly recorded concerning his questionable conduct. Mr. Harvey was discovered in his room at Stepney Green in a state of dismemberment and his throat, as described by the housekeeper, "having been bitten out." A medical examination concludes that Mr. Harvey was torn apart by hand and by no discernable instrument except brute and savage strength.

"Though animal attack is not ruled out, this writer did enter the room of the hapless victim and witnessed bloody handprints upon the wall, of a small and decidedly human individual.

"Mr. Harvey is not the only unfortunate to die in such a manner. Mr. Bark Blakesley of Camden Town was found at home in similar savaged state on the 22 February; Mrs. Sara Elliot in her Islington grocery store and parts of her in the flour barrel on the 28th. All had been rent apart. Their remains bore teeth marks and the bruises of having been forcibly handled, this as testified in the autopsy reports. Whether murdered by animal or by human hands, one must gravely consider that something reanimated is afoot in London, devoid of soul and capable of a single purpose: Death."

~

"You should pick a name for yourself," Jim said when Artifice lowered the paper. He inhaled and the cigarette between his teeth burned a third way to ash. "Any sort of moniker that takes your fancy. I'll be damned if I use the name Fall gave you."

"Why, Friend?" Artifice said. "Is it not a good name?"

"No. Only when you pick it. We surviving agents all picked ours. Then you'll know yourself sooner. You've questions, I bet. The moment I saw this case I knew the usual realisations agents must face would come swiftly to head."

"Has." She regarded him gravely. "What are we?"

"Asked like a true, Truth seeker! No wonder the Quaker women before you were put in brank's bridles. Well, we're not mindless carcasses. Much as the other papers would have us so. We are what we are, whatever 'we' are, and like newborn babes of developing intelligence and sentience, we eventually make of ourselves what we will. But to your real question: Are we as much puppets to our Commission, our strings pulled like those skinned cats and overworked horse? In some ways, yes. You gave solemn affirmation to obey. Your second life is theirs, not yours. Otherwise, we have autonomy. Thee is a Quaker, yes? Act like one. Take your own name and exercise thy second chance at becoming someone."

"Call me Art, Friend," she said. "It speaks to heart."

"'Art' it is. Now light me another, and I'll smoke it while you walk us to Whitechapel Market."

After feeding Jim another cigarette Art rose and picked him up. The beggar woman still glared at them.

"You're a very stupid goose," Jim said to her.

Art strolled on to the street and entered the hurl and burl of bodies, smells, noise, and traffic once more. The crowd had thickened though those on foot, hoof, or wheels quickly did their best to leave Art room. She glanced up at the sky. High above the city's haze the tiny ovals of airships glided. A horse nearly bumped into her. The driver cursed Art, but when she looked at him he stopped and hurriedly urged his horse around them.

Art stood on Fleet Street and turned her head for east and the distant top of St. Paul's Cathedral. Somehow she felt their destination lay beyond. If Jim knew otherwise, he would let her know. She hefted her walking stick. Her skirts were cut high enough that she needn't take hold of them. She moved swiftly.

Little by little she knew that she may awaken, whatever

knowledge left to her by the Secret Commission would come or she would rediscover it; whether she liked ginger beer or no, whether she wrote with her left or her right, or if she preferred the color red. Right then she knew she was not moving as one of her sex should; decorum, femininity, and humility she easily discarded. She ran, enjoying the power of her body and how when she exercised just a small part of her supernatural ability she could glide faster over the terrain, thus giving Jim a ride in her hand with minimum bumps and bruises. He laughed.

"Make way, make way!" he shouted. "Make way for the ghost!"

She could be a skinned cat that refused to die or a broken-necked horse galloping madly. She understood then that she was a spectre to those who saw her of what should never happen; unnatural, unknown, and unfathomable. She was Death walking. She ran swiftly down the road.

CHAPTER TWO

The narrow alleys of Whitechapel Market were busy; frightened animals were being driven underground to be slaughtered
in basements, their fresh dung caking the street. In the stalls
lining the small street, butchers were hanging all manner of
raw, dark meat, the cuts and portions unidentifiable. They laid
out tripe. Women with babies bartered loudly with the sellers.

"Ha ha! Road kill," Jim said, twisting in Art's hand to look at
the mysterious meat of one stall. Art paused in her walk to take
in the odd phrase.

"There's a bobby! He'll know where the deed was done," Jim
said, turning in her hand again. Art took a breath and set aside
her question. Her lack of understanding of some of Jim's queer
words could be due to lost memory, she thought. She cut a
path through a pack of running street boys and approached the
policeman laconically talking to a fish fryer.

Minutes later she was standing among other spectators who'd
come to gawk at the alley wall where the cat meat man had met
his end. Some of the blood had been cleansed; otherwise there
was nothing to look at but the bit of walk where Culver Drury
skinned his cats.

Some young men jostled Art and she firmly deterred a sly

hand entering the folds of her dress with the handle of her walking stick. The pickpocket smoothly withdrew with his accomplices.

"Such a loss!" Jim said loudly as he stared at the alley wall. "I can just imagine that innocent and poor man's horrible end. And for no good reason!"

"I 'eartily disagree," an old ragged woman said from her window behind them. She had a clear view of the alley. "Drury was a vicious li'l brute. Yew'll find no tears shed for the likes of 'im."

"Oh, come now." Art turned so that Jim could look at the woman. "Does anyone deserve to have their meat kill them?"

"If you'd seen 'ow he did it you'd say same," she said darkly. "They weren't mere meat to 'im."

"Then who spoke to him last," Jim asked in seriousness. "Who was here when it happened?"

The woman made to answer when her head tilted back. Her eyelids fluttered. Then a toothless smile broke upon her lined face.

"Mary 'ad a little lamb," she said pleasantly. "Fleece all white with snow. And ev'where that Mary went, the lamb was sure to go. I h'idn't see anyone, sir."

Art sensed something; a fleeting brush that passed like shadow between them and the woman. Though she still faced the window, she felt as if the shadow swung her around. Art shook her head to get her bearings.

"Thank you, madam. Art, a token for her help."

Art placed a few coins in the old woman's eager hand.

As they walked away, curious boys broke from the murder scene spectators and followed them.

"Something happened," Art said to Jim.

"Good! You've your senses. Gin dimmed Billy's. The woman back there had been mesmerized, and you felt a bit of the black spell still on her."

"I felt turned around. Myself and my thoughts."

"Think of how a bobby must have felt. Not sure why we didn't get a whiff of necromancy. Must've gone poof with the second death of the cats."

"You those Secret Inspectors?" a grinning boy next to Art suddenly asked. "You goin' to catch the warlock raisin' them killer animals?"

"No, we're going to ask him to tea! Maybe he'll bring back my dear beloved doggie!" Jim said.

"Nick Blackheart would've 'ad him by now! The Blackheart would've chopped 'is 'ead off! Whoosh!" said the ragged boy on the other side of Art. He cut the air with an imaginary sword.

"The old Nick is good, but we're taking care of this one!" Jim said.

Art paused when they arrived at a crossway that branched into three other alleys. She looked down at the boys tolerantly as they ran around them and whooped.

"The Secret Men 'ave nothin' on the Blackheart!" one boy scoffed.

"Blackheart, Blackheart, Blackheart!" they chanted. They laughed and ran.

"Ar! The Nick will always be more popular! Go watch some poor cow get pole axed, you little rascals!" Jim yelled after them.

"Where to now, Friend?" Art asked.

"The murdered teacher's," Jim sighed. "For we need to know what was resurrected that's not an animal."

Art sobered and scrutinized her surroundings. She saw nothing but the laundry lines of the poor who lived in the little alley. If she reached a main thoroughfare she might remember where Stepney Green was. She stepped beneath the dangling black stockings and wet shirts and followed her nose for the market.

"Friend, who is the Blackheart?" she asked.

Though Jim had no features Art felt he looked at her aghast.

"You don't know?" he said incredulously.

"Perhaps I never read penny dreadfuls."

"Nick Blackheart's not a penny dreadful hero or villain. She's real."

"She?" Art said. The Blackheart was becoming more peculiar by the minute.

"The latest Nick is. I believe she's the fifth. And very good at it too, been at it five years. But she's not been seen for months. Any of this giving you a ring?"

"A ring?" Art said in bafflement. "No, Friend."

"Fall made a mistake with your memories! It's essential you know this! Father Christmas?"

"Yes," Art said.

"Punch and Judy?"

"Yes."

"Arr! That Fall. I'll give you the beginning. Never mind, I'll give you the whole of it. Black arts in England had its time to grow. And be used foolishly. The first Nick Blackheart appeared around 1840, I believe, riding out to rid the countryside of supernatural muck gone amok. He became the monster killer. Was at it a good while and when he died his name and legacy was passed on; tricorne, mask, cloak, silver pistols and all. Dashing fellow. But the supernatural is not impressed by dashing. Nick after Nick came and each, in some horrifying fashion, went. And even with a Blackheart on duty it was not possible for every threat to be defeated. Thus it was when the fourth Blackheart perished and the plague of Devil Dogs nearly wiped out half the East End that Prince Albert decided evil must be harnessed in England's service to fight evil. And so the Secret Commission was born."

"If there's no sixth Blackheart the fifth must still be alive."

"Let's hope so. She first appeared on that big black horse of hers when the Devil Dogs were about to overrun and devour all of London. Drove them back in the—ha ha!—nick of time. Road kill for everyone! The poor ate heartily that night."

Art wasn't amused. Jim's very odd way of speaking seemed

further evidence of her lack of memory and the realisation of how much she didn't know disturbed her.

Jim continued, "While we agents were being created—and expiring faster than a Nick—the Blackheart rode on, dispatching horrors straightaway to hell. Truly an efficient woman. And dashing. I've never seen her myself. Would be nice when she returns, I'm due for a holiday."

Art ceased walking.

Something near was giving off a sensation. She felt it like a faraway lamp seen in the dark, but one that burned blackness not light and bloomed tendrils of subtle stench. Yet while the sensation made her skin crawl, it felt as familiar as the electrified eldritch energy she had awoken in at the Secret Commission.

"Hm," Jim murmured. "He's here."

Art moved swiftly under the laundry lines.

"Art, keep your distance and be silent!" Jim whispered urgently. "He mustn't become aware of us!"

She came to the end of the alley and held back to peer around the corner. A dark-haired man carrying a blanket-wrapped bundle was running through the shoppers among the street stalls.

"Too late! Art, after him!" Jim said.

She rounded the corner and pursued.

She was faster than the fleeing man, and despite the shoppers and carts in her way she easily overtook him. With confidence she grabbed for his shoulder when—

The world seemed to flip on its head. Art lost her footing, unable to sense up or down.

"Oh whammy," Jim said in disorientation as Art stumbled about. The dark-haired man turned and ducked into an entry that men were driving cattle into. A costerman near Art walked into a wall while a woman fell over her vegetable baskets. Several woozy people dropped and hugged the ground. Art kept to her feet but tilted dangerously near a fishmonger's fry.

"Watch it, watch it, hot oil!" Jim cried. "Now around; around, that's it. Now go, Art, into the building!" he encouraged once Art was faced in the right direction. She tried a few steps, found herself steadier, and ran.

The entry to below was blocked with two cows, and the men meant to herd them stood with blank expressions. Art didn't stop but took ghost form and passed through the wall. Jim hit it with a sharp crack and fell to the ground.

"DAMN IT, ART!" he yelled. Art re-emerged from the wall.

"Sorry Friend, I thought thee could pass!"

"Well, obviously I can't!"

She picked him up and pushed through the cows in the entryway.

Down the ramp was a large basement area—the slaughter floor. One cow already lay with its head cracked. The slaughter men stood transfixed, their long-handled pole axes loose in their hands. At the end of the room the dark-haired man waited with his back to Art.

She heard a scuffle and glanced up. The street boys had scurried to the ground level windows and were peering in, mouths open.

"Good sir," Jim said calmly as Art slowly moved forward. "Let's talk. We've questions. . . extraordinary things have been happening and. . . perhaps you've answers."

Art was halfway across the room when the dark-haired man stiffened. She thought she heard words but couldn't discern them. Something slipped from the blanket bundle he carried. It was the tiny foot of a child.

The slaughter man nearest her abruptly swung his pole ax.

Art quickly stepped aside. The ax head hit the floor with a resounding thud. Another slaughter man slowly moved forward, blocking her way. The dark-haired man exited quickly.

"Friends!" Art said. "Stand aside!"

"Art, they're mesmerized, they can't hear you!" Jim said.

"They're not of their mind!"

"I know that, just—kick them, push them, get us out of here!"

"I won't hurt th—"

A dull thud sounded as a pole ax buried itself in Art's back.

"ART!" Jim yelled.

Another pole ax connected with her middle. She doubled over and dropped Jim.

"Good God, like this, is it?!" he cried as he hit the slaughter floor. He rolled to a stop and saw the head of a pole ax hurtling down.

Art suddenly filled his vision. He heard a loud thud as she received the blow. She rose, grabbed the handle of the ax, and with a loud cry heaved it upwards. The motion flung the man wielding the ax up into the basement ceiling. He hit the rafters and then dropped to the ground. Jim saw another ax cut through the air, and Art met it with the one in her hand. She swung her arm back, the heads of the axes catching each other. The man who held the other weapon flew over her head and across the room.

"Art!" Jim yelled when she dropped her ax. Then he saw why. A weaponless slaughter man approached and threw a fist for her face. She blocked it with a forearm and punched the man squarely across his jaw. He spun around and collapsed on the floor next to Jim. Art then punched the fourth slaughter man, one fist to his stomach and the other fist swinging up to crack against his chin. The man dropped his pole ax and crumbled.

Jim heard boys cheering.

Hooves fast approached. An animal bellowed. Art staggered above Jim, dazed. He wanted to close his eye sockets, ready to feel a hoof smash him. The floor rumbled and the hoof he expected appeared above. Art grabbed the animal's horned head with both arms and twisted her body. She used the animal's momentum to throw it over, slamming it to the ground. The steer let out a plaintive moo. Art let go and shakily crawled to

Jim. She picked him up.

"My hat! My hat, Art!" Jim said. She found it, put it on his head, and straightened it. The animal was still mooing.

"Art, kill it?" he said. He didn't want the steer to rise again and gore her.

"No more," she gasped. She fumbled around until she retrieved her stick. She stumbled for the ramp and basement opening.

When Art emerged she felt there were several things torn inside of her. Were she human she would be vomiting blood, but since that hadn't happen yet she felt she could manage consciousness for a little while. She leaned against a wall and tried to move the hand with the walking stick behind her. She needed to get at the pole ax stuck in her back.

Her vision clouded and one of her legs gave way.

When her eyes cleared, she thought she did well saving them from a fall because Jim was still in her hand, her walking stick was supporting her, and she'd only fallen to one knee. However, Jim was berating her.

"Art, while you were nodding a street rascal relieved you of your purse! A slew of boys came running and—good God, woman! You've a pole ax in your back!"

"Friend. . . the men. I hit them too hard," Art gasped.

"What? Just eat something, hurry! Eating will heal you! I thought I saw turnips! Potatoes? There's fried fish over there! And—what's this?"

The street boys ran up to where Art knelt. The leader held Art's coin purse.

"We snatched it back for you." He grinned as he handed it to her. "And took our fee, too."

"Keep it, you've a task," Jim said. "You saw what Art did to the slaughter men, right? Go back in. Any that need a doctor, give them that."

"Sir," the boy said, instantly serious. He nodded and ran into the building with his companions.

"My thanks, Friend," Art said.

"Now Art, eat something, damn it. Before I make someone force turnips into you."

She stood with a jerk, her body trembling. She was surrounded by stalls of hanging red meat, frying fish, whelks being boiled—none of it called to her.

"DAMN IT, ART!" Jim cried.

She quickly lashed out with her stick. A man was hurrying by with his barrow full of live whelks and she hooked it. She stared at the shells and they began to shake. She opened her arms.

The whelks flew from the barrow and entered her body. They rattled within her as she drew the flesh out and absorbed the creatures. When she was done the empty shells dropped at her feet. The pole ax fell from her back with a thud.

The whelks seller grabbed hold of his empty barrow and ran.

"Wait, man, don't you want payment?" Jim called after him.

Art set her stick to the ground. She walked. She was still shaky.

"Art, there's more over there."

"No," she said. "Raw."

"Who has live whelks?!" Jim cried. "Raw fish, oysters, eels, c'mon now!"

"Here, here, here!" A nervous man said, waving them to his stall. He had uncooked whelks in a basket.

"Do you accept the pin of the Secret Commission? Know what that means, right?" Jim asked. When they neared, Jim spat out a black shield shaped pin on a black ribbon. The seller nodded vigorously.

"Yes, yes, yes," he said. Taking an empty shell, he placed the pin against it and it began to smoke. The image of the shield was burned into the surface.

"Good man! Take that to the Secret Commission's payer. Art, eat now."

Art drew the whelks into her body and repeated her harvesting process. Soon a pile of empty shells was at her feet.

"Ah! Your colour has returned. A nicer shade of pale. Let's see if you're whole."

She felt better, almost as new. She set Jim down on the seller's cart so he could look at her back.

"Good God, woman. You're about to split the seams of your back, and you've lost your sleeves already. Oh, and there are two large holes, but looks like all wounds are gone."

Art glanced at her shoulders and realised Jim was right. Her exertion had burst the seams of her bodice and the sleeves were sagging. Her pale skin was showing. Many among the market crowd who gathered around them were pointing and murmuring at her state of undress.

"I've learned that when my partners end up unclothed whilst in the line of duty, the attention drawn to their dishabille always gets in the way of investigation," Jim said in humour. "Billy went into a furnace once, came back out, had all his hair still but his clothes were gone. And I won't tell you about Harold's escapade. Let's get you sewn up."

"But the re-animationist," Art said.

"Will have to wait. Else you'll be battling him in your undergarments."

~

Queries at the market led Art and Jim to a seamstress nearby. She lived in a ground floor room, so Art rapped at the open window and stepped back. When the woman, thin and sallow-faced, looked out, she gasped at the sight of them.

"Friend," Art gently said before the woman could retreat. "I am Art and this is Jim Dastard, agents of the Secret Commission. I have need of thy skills. My garment must be mended and quickly."

"Well, I, well," said the flustered woman.

"Madam, your name if I may ask?" Jim said.

"Oh, Jane Finch, sir," she said.

"Mrs. Finch. You can see my partner is in a state of embarrassment. We must restore her respectability so that she doesn't, YOU know," he said with emphasis. If he had eyebrows Art felt he might wag them. "Attract that element of men? The male pests?" he added in a loud whisper.

"Oh, Mr. Dastard! Yes! I do understand! Please come in!"

Art entered Jane's tiny room and saw the one bed and lone candle used to light the space. Two young girls sat with needles in hand. Shirts were in their lap. Their little bodies were bent from hunching over their work, and their faces were as sallow as their mother's. Jane was just then looking at the Secret Commission pin between Jim's teeth. She shook her head.

"But, I can't leave to collect it. We've work, and my girls. . . " Jane said.

Art observed the table. The family was labouring over piecework; piles of shirts needed buttonholes stitched into them.

I know how to do that, Art thought.

"We'll buy thee needed things—if thee would mend my dress," she offered.

"That—that we can do," Jane agreed.

"My Friend will do the purchasing. Will thy daughters take him?"

"Art, what am I to buy?" Jim asked.

"Thread," she said to him. "For she supplies her own. As many as the girls can carry. Buttons." She saw their shopping basket and picked it up. "Needles if needed. Candles for their late night work, and an oil lamp to better aid them. Tea and food," she added in a low voice. She turned to the children. "Now, which is brave enough to take this man from me?" she coaxed with a smile.

"I don't bite," Jim said. "Though I'm known to nibble— num num, delicious fingers!"

His jest made the girls giggle. The older one bravely held out her hands.

When Jim and the children had left, Art set her stick aside and pulled off her gloves. She quickly unhooked her bodice from her skirt. She unbuttoned it and shrugged out of the damaged sleeves. The seams along the back were splitting. Once she pulled the garment off, she was in her fitted white underbodice, the well-developed musculature of her white shoulders and arms revealed.

"Well, I!" Jane said under her breath. "Oh my!"

"Friend?"

"Oh. Nothing. You've holes in your undergarments as well. They're. . . stained. How did this happen?"

"A fight, Friend. Are the blood stains unsightly?"

"Blood? Well, if it is that. . . no, not so unsightly."

Art reached behind her, realising she didn't know the state of her corset. She had just thrown a large animal—did she break the corset's boning while doing so? She felt the tear the pole ax had made in her under-bodice and then Jane's hands joining hers, feeling for her corset beneath.

"Your corset's whole, despite what made the tear," Jane said in surprise. "Why the boning gives; I don't think that's steel. And what a strange design! Between it's like armour plating. Lovely, the way it's arranged." She traced the lines with her fingers. "I bet it's patented. But your bustle's in sad shape. It's metal?"

Art heard it creak as Jane experimentally pushed on her bottom.

"If sat on properly it's meant to collapse," Jane said with admiration. "Another interesting design! Your dress is beautiful work."

"'Tis. And 'twill have to do," Art said. "A task was left undone we must return to. I need only be presentable."

"Then I'll mend this straight away."

She took the bodice from Art, chose a needle and thread from her basket, and sat down near the window. Art picked up the first shirt needing buttonholes and claimed the seat of one of the daughters. She picked up the needle that had been set aside and rapidly began stitching, her white fingers a blur of motion. Jane stared at Art's speed, then forced her attention back to the bodice. She sewed as fast as she could, repairing seams and closing tears. The pile of finished shirts grew.

When Jim and the girls returned, he was sitting in the shopping basket and talking animatedly. The girls held sweets along with the supplies. Art raised her head and smiled at them. She accepted the new lantern from the younger daughter, prepared it, and stood to hang it. As she did so, her muscles flexed.

"Extraordinary!" Jim exclaimed. The girls stared up at Art, mouths agape.

She turned around and looked at Jim curiously.

"Mrs. Finch, I hope your stitches hold, but it may not be possible," Jim said. "Art needs a proper measuring. The dressmaker didn't take into account that she has a physique that needs, ah, expansion."

Art looked at Jim more while the girls giggled.

"Oh, why tiptoe around it?" Jim said. "You've just punched out grown men and thrown a steer! You'll ride bicycles next! To put it delicately, you're quite unsexed. But I for one, am impressed."

"Unsexed!" Jane exclaimed. "For a lady perhaps, but women fight, Mr. Dastard! And I don't mean the Blackheart."

"Like when drinking, Mrs. Finch?" Jim said jovially.

"That and when dealing with the men some have! And oh! Them battles where the working women hold their street!"

"You're right Mrs. Finch, God bless the good English woman who has her dukes ready to defend her honor and hearth. Art is done up so finely I forget she's a Clydesdale."

Jane laughed. "It's a wonder, sir. A Quaker fighting! It's sin to them."

A shadow crossed Art's face and she grew pensive. She summoned a smile for the children and bent forward.

"I shall take him now. Show thy mother thy purchases."

While they did so, Art set Jim on the table. She turned him to face her.

"I am Quaker," she said quietly. "Yet I was a criminal."

Jim scrutinized her a while.

"I was waiting for you to fully realise that," he finally said.

"I am Quaker," she repeated.

"I doubt you were a martyr. The Church has other things to think about than drowning or burning your sort anymore. You're in the Secret Commission because criminals are used to catch other criminals; this is the mission."

"I fought," Art whispered. "I fought well. What kind of criminal was I?"

"No. Don't ask. Whatever you think you were, leave it."

She didn't answer, her pale eyes distant.

"This must be that famous Quaker silence!" Jim exclaimed. "What a sound! Now Art, listen to me. Don't get confused. And know that you're not the only one to have gone through this. What you were is not what you are now. You're new, Art. A new kind of woman and yes, a new kind of Quaker. If you must have thoughts about it, those deep Quaker thoughts, do them later. We have a job to get done."

"Aye," she said. "We do."

She rose and retrieved her bodice from Jane and began dressing.

"Art," Jim said.

She looked at him.

"The fact that you are violent is deeply appreciated," he said. "Because had you not been, I'd be fragments on that slaughter room floor."

She smiled. "My thanks," she softly said.

CHAPTER THREE

Art walked the side streets near Whitechapel Market in new-ly-mended clothes, conspicuously a head taller than the rest of the women and some men who stood in doorways or dared to stroll near her. Children were more oblivious to her presence and ignored her while playing games. She wore a monocle. Jim was no longer in her hand but seated at Jane Finch's sill with a lit candle inside him. He wore a matching monocle and through the glasses' bewitched connection was able to see all that she saw.

"Feel anything yet?" he asked, his voice sounding in her ear.

"No, Friend," she said. She'd patiently answered the same question for the past half hour. The tools of "linked gazing" and "far-speaking" invented by the Commission were impres-sive but were gradually revealing their ability to annoy. Jim de-cided on this course of action so that Art would be free to use her ghost ability.

She crossed a street before Jim could direct her to and en-tered another small warren where women were washing. They were using tapping pipes to siphon steam power from the underground pumping engines. Little boys and girls tended the boiling taps that instantly heated the water brought in buckets. The women talked animatedly as they worked their washer boards, faces and hands red from the hot water and steam. Some glanced up at Art and eyed the elegant figure she made.

The monocle had been issued to Art at the Secret Commission and kept pinned in her dress pocket. To her eye it was mere glass and did not enhance her vision. Jim's comments while far-speaking proved that he could indeed see directly out of her monocle. She, however, could not see out of his, which was just as well because Jim was unable to do anything more than sit. Stored in Jim's top hat were several small candles of different colors. Slow burning, he had said, and each of different supernatural purpose. He explained the brown one she had pulled out at his request back at Jane Finch's room.

"The spell is inherent in the candle. Brown is for communication. When you've a bit of its wax in your ear and the candle is lit inside me, I can speak to you. And hear you in turn. Simple."

"I can hear thy words with the wax in my ear?" Art said.

"Yes."

"And thee can hear my words, yet I've not eaten of the wax."

"No, you don't have to eat any wax."

"Certain?"

"Yes!"

Thus, she was walking about with a bit of wax in her ear and Jim's voice somehow speaking to her. True to what he said, he was able to hear her also. She wondered if mad people who heard voices experienced them just as she did, because she was presently conversing with Jim and looking equally insane.

"Your circling must be thorough, Art. It's like casting a net. I doubt a man carrying such a large bundle intended to travel far."

"Did thee see what was in the blanket? 'Twas a child. I saw its tiny foot."

"No. . . I missed that."

She thought about it.

"The child was the eldritch presence," she said.

"If it were a recent resurrection. . . yes."

Art emerged from the alley full of washerwomen and into a thoroughfare lined with furniture and old clothing shops. She stopped in surprise. Across the street stood the woman she'd seen in the Secret Commission lobby, but she was no longer wearing a mask. The woman saw Art as well, and her expression gave Art pause because not only did the woman appear to be shocked at the sight of her, but almost wrathful.

The woman's dark hair was neatly pinned back. She wore no hat or gloves, and clutched a black book to her bosom. An austere, high-collared, long black coat draped over her skirts. Her spectacles did not hide the intensity of her incredulous gaze.

"Art, there's something you should know about that eldritch feeling," Jim said in her ear.

"Friend," she said, acknowledging him. She turned away from the woman's disturbing attention and continued walking. For some reason the gaze upset her.

"We agents all have the same signature—that thing you sense. I'm sure when you first saw me you felt something of the kind."

"I did."

"And we're not the only agents in town. You'll stumble across a duo soon enough. So-called magic users also abound. Many are charlatans. You could pack a train with the lot. But a few have real power. It's in the feel of them that you'll be able to tell. You must learn how to distinguish between all of us; agents, supernaturalists, and the evil we fight."

Art glanced behind her; the woman in black had crossed the street and was following, her blue eyes boring holes in Art's back.

"How am I to discern threat?" she asked.

"Oh, that. Well, if something or someone wants to kill you,

of course."

"Very well," Art said. She turned a corner and in ghost form rushed through the building's shops to come around the woman in black.

When she reappeared behind the woman her quarry unexpectedly spun, book in hand. Startled, Art stepped back.

"No harm," Art said, raising her hands and walking stick.

"Your name!" the woman demanded. She stepped forward. Art stepped back again. She felt pinned by the woman's stare.

"Thine's," Art demanded in return.

Passers-by hurried around them while they measured each other.

Art had no doubt; the arched brows, the cheeks, lips and eyes, this was the same face she had seen in the Secret Commission lobby, but repurposed with a steel jaw and unsettlingly piercing regard.

"Did thee visit the Secret Commission today?" Art asked. She tried to make the query sound polite, but it came out uncertain.

"No," the woman said, briefly startled. "What are you?"

"An artificial ghost," Art said more firmly. "In service to the Secret Commission. Now thee. Thy name?"

"Yours first," the woman ordered.

"They call me Artifice, Friend," Art answered patiently. "Though I've taken the name Art."

To Art's surprise and dismay, her words seemed to wound the woman deeply. Art saw grief then anger manifest in her face.

"You certainly are," the woman said bitterly, backing away. She abruptly left.

"Well," Dastard said in Art's ear as she watched the woman's quickly retreating back. "You've disappointed someone."

Art slowly turned around and resumed walking.

"Art, to your left. Still making our circle, remember."

She obeyed and continued down a small dark street, avoiding the center gutter and its sewage. The cobblestoned surface bulged slightly from trapped gases beneath. A sailor and gaudi-ly-dressed woman were intimately engaged in a darkened door-way, but upon seeing her they moved apart and hurried away. Further down, two more women with painted faces noticed her and discreetly retreated.

"Are there those who actively hate us?" Art asked.

"A movement or organization you mean? Honestly, you would think so, but I've been at this from the infancy of the Commission and nothing comes to mind. There was opposi-tion in the beginning, especially with the Blackheart around. But it was mostly mud slung in the newspaper editorials."

"I don't know what just happened," Art said.

"Well, I saw the whole thing and I believe it was personal, Art."

Art stopped walking.

"Yes, I think you met someone from your past. We'll cele-brate it later. Back to hunting."

"Will this happen often?" Art asked. If she were so hated for whoever she once was, she didn't think she could bear it.

"Depends. But even the most quiet of former lives has histo-ry. All my partners had their pasts catch up with them. There's good that comes of it and bad. Well, mostly bad, and from what I've seen it always overwhelms. Remember what I said about confusion. Keep focused, think later. That woman is gone now, and perhaps you won't meet again. There's only the task at hand."

"Aye, Friend. My thanks for thy words."

"Words are what I have," Jim said. "Art, why did you turn just then? You're about to walk into a brothel."

Art stopped. She was indeed about to enter a tenement where a large bully stood just within the door, watching her, and women in states of loose dress lounged at the window. The brothel-keeper strode out, a wide smile on her broad face.

"Lost are yeh? Come in for a rest, yeh must be thirsty," she said kindly.

Art ignored the woman. While the brothel-keeper continued to coax her, Art gazed down the small street she thought she had been following. She took a step in its direction.

And found herself facing the brothel again. This time she was closer to the entrance. The women in the window stared at her as if she had performed an antic.

"Can't you see 'er badge, she's one o' those unnatural inspectors! What are you tryin', Sal?" said one of the women at the window, laughing nervously.

"Shut it!" Sal hissed at the woman. She had Art by the arm and spoke sweetly. "Yer havin' troubles, dearie. Let us help. Come in."

"Friend, did thee see what happened?" Art said to Jim. She spied the shadow of the bully as he waited behind the door-frame.

"Yes," Jim answered thoughtfully. "They nearly had you. Try 'up.'"

Art took ghost form, slipping from the brothel-keeper's grasp, and flew up. She abruptly felt the burning flame of eldritch power, dark and foul, emanating in the building across from the brothel. The flame became several flickers and moved. A dirty broken window was before her, and she saw the dark swift shapes of small children pass. She flew forward. A man stepped before the window. Dark-haired and bearded, he stared at her with wild eyes. He appeared to be speaking. She missed the window and smacked the wall in solid form. She fell two stories below.

When she came to, the bully was dragging her to the brothel. Sal hurriedly worked the buttons of Art's bodice.

Art took to her feet, shrugging out of the man's grip. Her stick was still in her hand. She used it to sweep Sal away while her free hand grabbed the bully's throat. She raised him in the air, choking him.

"Art, they were about to strip you, but you're all right now," Jim said quickly in her ear.

"I am," Art said. She slowly brought the choked bully back down to his feet.

"You weren't unconscious long, but our quarry has a gift for escape," Jim said. "If you can't feel him then he's long gone."

Art shoved the large man away. He doubled over, holding his throat. She glanced up. An airship glided by in the hazy sky visible between the buildings. There was nothing near that felt remotely supernatural.

"Yes Friend, he's gone," she soberly confirmed. She strolled purposefully for the brothel door and entered.

Once inside she rapped randomly on the wall with the handle of her walking stick. The noise attracted the ones in the rooms above. Women in states of undress emerged and peered fearfully down the staircase. If their clients were present, they kept out of sight.

"Who would like to leave?" Art called up to them. Suddenly her badge glowed.

"Art. I'm getting a communication," Jim said in her ear. "It's the Commission. You'll see their signal as your badge giving a light. Touch it and you'll receive their message."

"I'm occupied, Friend."

"I can see that. I'll take the communiqué, but you'll have to stop your horseplay with these ladies. Return post-haste and pick me up."

"Yes, Friend." Art turned to leave.

Three women hastily ran down the stairs. They were painted, disheveled, and more or less dressed.

"We're comin'. Take us out," one said to Art excitedly. The angry brothel-keeper blocked the door.

"We've a contract! They signed it and can't break it! You take them and the police will just return the bitches, they're my property!" Sal screeched.

"Oh, shut it! You'll send your minders to follow us anyway," a second woman said. "Take us out, now," she then said to Art. Art firmly pushed Sal aside and walked out the door. Jim chuckled in her ear.

Art escorted the women back to Jane Finch's where she retrieved Jim. He reminded her to button up her opened bodice. Then after convincing Jim to spit out the few coins he reserved for emergencies, Art escorted the women to an omnibus headed for the Strand.

"We thought you might lead us to a Midnight Mission," one of the women said playfully. They boarded eagerly with their fare in hand.

"Thee are grown women," Art said to them. "Agree to one thing."

"What's that," one woman asked, leaning forward.

"Be free and keep thy earnings for thyself. Work for that keeper no longer."

"Done," the woman cried, and her companions heartedly agreed. Art grabbed an old woman who tried to board the omnibus and lifted her out.

"Not thee," Art said to the minder who had been following them. "Nor thee," she said to a young furtive girl Art quickly removed by the scruff. The women on board laughed as the omnibus pulled away, gleeful to have left behind the keeper's spies.

"Art, they'll probably end up back in that harridan's clutches," Jim said as they watched the omnibus depart. "Especially when she has the police arrest them for stealing or some such. You cannot make a habit of this Quaker charity! We're agents, not a rescue society. This spot of social work has delayed us enough!"

"My apologies, Friend," Art said as she walked them quickly down the crowded thoroughfare of Bishopsgate. Her destination was the nearest train trestle; the tracks ran above their heads. "But I don't know why we're leaving.

The re-animationist is here."

"Perhaps he still is. We must go learn more. He's two for two, and when you encounter him a third time it better be with superior knowledge."

"I should have questioned the brothel-keeper," Art said in self-chastisement.

"What a snare that was, she was obviously paid. But you would have gotten a "lamb with fleece as white as snow" for your trouble, so never mind. Will I have to dissuade you of rescue in the future?"

"Friend. . . what I did, I hadn't charitable intention," Art confessed.

"What?" Jim cried. "You took those ladies out of spite? Oh yes, hit the harridan in her pockets! Better than wrecking the place with your bare hands, I bet, ha ha!"

"I had that uncharitable thought."

She found a trestle that she could climb. She ignored the gawkers on the street as she mounted the ladder. With great focus she walked out upon the overhang above the raised tracks.

"Right," Jim said, excited. "This is something I've always wanted to do since Harold's passing. Let's hop the train."

"Will thee know the station?" Art asked.

"Yes. We're headed for the peaceful surroundings of Bloomsbury. A fresh kill somberly awaits us."

A train soon rushed beneath them. Art stepped out and dropped. She knew by the speed that she wouldn't keep her feet and trusted that she would stop their roll before they fell off the car.

~

The street in Bloomsbury was very quiet, the houses neat and orderly. One home had several hansom cabs and a hackney carriage before it. Onlookers stood on the walk and murmured amongst themselves while a policeman stoically looked on.

A penny-farthing rested against a post. Art and Jim strolled up the walk, and several spectators backed away. If the duo inspired more gossip, it was possibly commentary on Art's finery, which appeared rough and a little sooty. A mustached inspector stood outside making a thoughtful statement to listening journalists. Upon seeing Art and Jim he moved away.

"Mr. Dastard," he greeted.

"Inspector Risk! My new partner, Art, the artificial ghost," Jim introduced. "Well man, what do we have?"

"A dead wife, a dead baby, and the man of the house with a mangled throat but he's still living. C'mon."

Art followed Inspector Risk into the house.

The dead woman lay in the parlour near the fireplace, her torso ravaged and her throat torn out. Small, silver-framed oval portraits lined the mantle, all of solemn little girls. Art looked down at the body and carefully stepped so that she didn't disturb the scene. Tiny bloody footprints stained the carpet.

"A barefoot child. Was it found?" Jim asked.

"Checked every door and drawer. We'd ask the husband, but he's currently in a faint," Risk said flatly.

"She didn't struggle," Jim said as Art tilted him to look down at the dead woman. "I didn't catch her name."

"Mrs. Harriet Hillings."

Art noticed the small bloody handprint on the wallpaper by the fireplace. She knelt to look and placed her own hand next to it, taking its measure.

"The babe was three," she murmured.

"Yes. Well, the Hillings recently lost their three-year old girl to a terrible illness. Learned it from the kitchen maid. I'll not say yet that their daughter made these prints. The child's buried," Risk said.

"You'd better see that's still true," Jim said. "Art, let's go up to the nursery."

She found the staircase, and while ascending it Mr. Hillings was carried out of the dining room on a stretcher by two men. They headed for the front door. He lay pale and in a stupor, his throat heavily bandaged.

Risk watched as they carried him out. "Useless," he muttered.

"So he fought the creature off, Risk?" Jim asked.

"Until he tells us himself, we can only assume that's the case. He got the attacker off him and managed to shut himself in a closet. The kitchen maid, Mary Evers, ran for the police when she thought the attacker finally gone. She didn't know what happened in the rest of the house and didn't know Mr. Hillings was still living."

"And when the bobbies arrived?" Jim said.

"He tumbled out and that's how they found him," Risk said.

"Up we go, Art," Jim said. She continued up the stairs.

More blood was smeared on the walls like a small child had been fingerpainting. The nursery entrance was clearly marked with little handprints where the door was pushed aside.

"I'll look," Jim said. "Just put your arm in. I won't be long."

Art didn't protest. She slowly brought her arm around until Jim told her he was done.

"Worse than downstairs," Jim said as they descended. "Let's find the kitchen maid. I bet she's in the kitchen."

The maid sat with a policeman keeping her company. She was a round-faced young woman with chubby cheeks and a rumpled uniform. Her hands were clasped upon the table but her thumbs rubbed against each other fretfully.

"Hello Mary," Jim greeted. The maid jumped. "Oh! Didn't mean to startle you. I'm Jim Dastard, and my silent friend here is Art. Excuse our rough looks. We've been chasing evil all day. But tough day for you, hasn't it been? Don't you wish it were done!"

"Oh sir! You don't know the half of it!" Mary cried.

"Mary, I know you've things to tell us. Say Art, that's a lovely lit cook stove. Ah, wood! Set me on the top, I've not eaten since morning."

Art did so. With Jim on the black stove he sat closer to Mary. Art silently stepped back and watched Jim converse with the young woman.

"Well I was 'ere, sir," Mary said to Jim. "Delivery just come, and I was cutting the vegetables and such. I'd prepared the stove for a bit of laundry boiling. I heard Mrs. Hillings answer the front door and give a most happy cry! It surprised me sir, there'd been much sadness in this house. I thought perhaps a good friend or relative had come who cheered her greatly. So I kept working here, and then. . . and then." Mary ceased speaking and swallowed.

"What did you hear?" Jim asked gently.

"Oh, the most. . . oh sir, the missus. It was like when her li'l girl died and her grief come tearing out of her. She wailed," Mary whispered. "She wailed 'n screamed 'n wailed."

"What did you do?" Jim asked.

"Oh, I stuffed myself into the larder, sir," she said. "I don't know how I managed it. And I heard more 'orribleness. It just kept going on. I nearly lost my mind, but I told myself, "Mary, if you want to live you ought to make a run." So I did. The scullery door never seemed so far, sir."

"You did well, Mary. You did superbly," Jim said. "God bless you, girl. Now I must ask: What was Mrs. Hillings's state of mind this morning? Or even last night or several days previous? What would you say her temperament was like?"

"Oh sir, now that you've said," Mary said thoughtfully. "She seemed expectant! That was yesterday. It was a real change, she'd been so sad. I thought maybe she'd 'eard some good news. I mean, she didn't even go out shopping today, and she always does. And then when she answered the door. . . that's what I thought it was."

"It was reasonable to think, Mary, it was. Have you seen a young man visit Mrs. Hillings, perhaps? Today or on another day. He would have looked a bit of a swell. Handsome, with dark hair and beard, neatly trimmed. A devilish fellow. Like one of those painters or poets or other idlers who haunt the Strand."

"No sir. I'd notice someone like that."

"Would you know if the missus made or kept any interesting appointments lately? Maybe she mentioned going out to meet someone," Jim said.

"Oh sir, she hasn't, not to me anyways. Mrs. Hillings liked to go shopping in the West End every day. Lookin' at the windows was her passion. She also took tea and luncheon down there too. That's all I know."

Jim thanked Mary for her time, and Art picked him up. He'd absorbed enough of the stove's fire to leave it glowing embers. When they emerged from the kitchen, Risk was in the hall, thumbing through a ladies' ivory-cased day planner.

"Retrieved from her desk," Risk said. "Her appointments say: hairdresser, dressmaker, Ladies' Club. The occasional butcher's shop. And everyday is shopping. And tea."

"A diagnostician, a spiritualist, a clairvoyant, a magician— anything?" Jim asked.

"Not a one," Risk said. "Who was that fellow you were describing?"

"The re-animationist," Jim said. "Art and I were on his trail today. I'll send you an artist's rendering on the morrow."

"Your artist is good," Risk said. "Persuade her to make a living at it."

"She makes more doing other things," Jim said. "For now."

"Friend Risk, was a department store name written down?" Art asked.

Risk peered at the elegant planner in his large hand. "Always the same one," he said. "Liberty's."

"My thanks," Art said.

～

Art left Jim in Risk's hands while they talked of other matters. She decided to exit the house. Once she stepped out on
the porch, several of the journalists ignored the policeman and
rushed forward to speak to her. They introduced themselves
and peppered her with queries. She noticed one who didn't.

The young woman in the leather half mask stood before her
again, this time so close that Art could see the tiny metal studs
and painted decoration upon the leather. Along the edge that
fitted against the woman's eye were delicately painted blue
flowers.

Forget-me-not, Art thought. She looked at the woman, who
smiled, her eyes wide with secret delight. Art felt something
pressed into her hand. The woman's gloved fingers were unac-
countably warm. They left a silver engraved card. The masked
woman winked. She then turned and ran.

Art took to the air, rising above the other journalists to see
where the woman went. She was running madly for the penny-farthing leaning against the post, her dark hair come loose
under her hat. Her skirts were cut high enough to show the
ankles of her boots. She jumped, one boot landing on a step
upon the wheel's frame and the other kicking off the ground.
She mounted the seat in side-saddle. Her foot hit the treadle to
accelerate the wheel. The big wheel promptly pitched upon a
pothole and sent the woman over the handlebars.

Aghast, Art fell to the ground and rushed through the journalists in ghost form. They cried out and scattered. But the
woman was already up, having tumbled to her feet, and was
rolling her wheel once more. Art heard her laugh, the sound
gay and free. Her hat was askew. She leapt into the seat of her
wheel and sped away.

"Art, what are you doing? Everyone's looking this way like
they've seen a ghost," Jim said. Inspector Risk held him. They
both laughed heartily. Art retrieved Jim from Risk and hurriedly
bade the inspector farewell.

"Art, you all right?" Jim asked as she walked away. She looked at the card in her hand. It simply said: HELIA SKYCOURT.

"Friend, who is Helia Skycourt?" Art asked.

"A journalist," Jim said. "You read her article this morning."

"Yes, but I've just met her," Art said. "And she is. . . a surprise."

"Was she here? That's no surprise, she can smell dark works anywhere."

"She rode away on a wheel but gave me her card."

"About time one of those journalists contacted us! I've never met her, though she's followed our cases plenty. I like her writing. Not so florid, that Miss Skycourt—Lady Skycourt, since you're asking. She's aristo. And is quite an advocate for things supernaturalist. What else. A competing velocipedestrienne. She does it side-saddle, can you imagine? A lunatic—"

"What?" Art said, startled.

"Yes! Looney! She's been in and out of asylums since a girl. Doesn't affect her wordsmithing, she's a wicked pen! Ask the suffragettes, or the Temperance Society, or the Society of Psychical Research. Heh heh! That was a read—"

"Friend, speak plainly," Art pleaded.

"I am! She's a madwoman. Has a very unfortunate past. It's also why she wears the mask. I don't know firsthand of the real matter. Anyone can wag a tongue, and before you know it you've dropped ten babies instead of one. It's person-to-person where you'll get truth. Or at least part of it. It's good you've her card."

She examined it again, then tucked it safely away.

"Truth then, why would thee call her mad?" she asked.

"Hm. An excellent question," Jim said thoughtfully. "Well. With pen and body she runs pell-mell. Do you know what she called the Blackheart, the poor's defender from the supernatural? "The Blaggard." Nick's opponents took up the slur with glee! Helia Skycourt has enemies, she's ruined people, and she doesn't care. She seems bent towards personal destruction."

Art recalled the happy light she had seen in Helia's eyes.

"I did not feel that from her," she said. They arrived at the tracks that ran through Bloomsbury. Art placed Jim on her walking stick and ascended the train trestle's ladder by one hand.

"Then good," Jim said. "I'd prefer to be wrong." She walked them across the archway.

"Has she a sister?" Art asked cautiously. She wondered if Helia's madness might be of a dual personality. If so, the other side of her was intimidating.

"Why yes, Lady Helene Skycourt, the adventuress! Both are unmarried, so Helene will inherit Skycourt Industries—and her family's earldom. They make airships."

An adventuress, Art thought. Perhaps Lady Helene was having a personal adventure disguised as an ascetic, wandering the East End. The aristocracy, if she recalled correctly, were known to slum for the thrill of it.

"They are twins," she said.

"Hm? Yes, twins. Here comes our iron steed!"

As the train roared below, Art tucked Jim close and jumped.

⁓

It was evening; their ride was short. Their next route was closer than the East End. They hopped off the train before it submerged into the tunnel systems. Art walked them to Fleet Street. The street was more crowded than before, thunderous with the sound of hooves and wheels. The front of the newspaper offices was congested with hansom cabs, carts, and broughams. Art found herself looking furtively for a penny-farthing.

"Always submitting their advertisements and letters to the editor at the last hour," Jim said. "I usually have a woman deliver mine. A pretty one. Gives my letters a leg up."

"I've an idea," Art said to Jim. "Friend Hillings liked to shop. 'Tis ritual with women of her class. Let us go to her favourite store tomorrow. Those who know her will be there, and we may hear helpful things. The papers will inspire talk in the morning."

"When they report her death," Jim said. "That is an excellent suggestion. And I hate it because it means having to endure tea amongst the dull, nothing-to-do harpies. The shop assistants at Liberty's are lovely girls, though. It's a plan, then."

They reached the great hall of the Gaiety Theatre. Art walked the length of the walk outside, the attendees, loiterers, beggars, and flower sellers making room for her to pass. She and Jim found the women Jim was to meet. They spotted the two smartly-dressed ladies being talked to by a policeman.

"Here's our man," one of the women exclaimed. "So you can leave us be!" They quickly approached Art and Jim.

"Hildy! Jenny! This is Art, my new partner and a ghost," Jim said. The women politely greeted Art, then accepted Jim from her hands.

"Jenny, I'll need you to sketch a portrait for me later," Jim said.

"Oh sir, I've just taken a new position. I've hats to make in the morning!" Jenny said. "I mustn't wake up late for it or I'll be dismissed."

"Now Jen, I pay you well for your drawings. And for your other charms. Hildy will make sure you'll get to the milliner's, won't you, Hildy? I'll buy you those watercolour paints you've wanted," Jim coaxed.

Jenny seemed pleased with the offer, and Jim prompted them to turn him so he could speak to Art.

"Well my young friend, congratulations!" Jim said to Art. "You've survived your first night, pole axed and all! I think you deserve a show, and I'd like to treat you to one."

"Kind Friend, my thanks. But I've learned much today and feel I need my thinking time."

"Well, if you must retreat, I should let you know that

lodgings are not assigned; we agents find what suits since we're not human. Keep that in mind if a cozy bed is not really to your liking. Billy was perfectly happy inhabiting people's coal bins and scaring the maids in the morning. Now, are you sure you won't join us? A grand playbill is promised!"

"Friend, I must decline again."

"Quaker! Canst thou put a l'il song and dance in thy heart?"

"I can, but not tonight. Personal matters need tendering."

"Mysterious! Well tell me it later. Unless it's boring."

"Before thee goes, how do I replenish my purse?" Art asked.

"I should have told you. That badge on your chest works like my pin. But the payer at the Commission building will issue you funds. Third floor. And they'll be there, because death and mayhem never rests. Squeeze the misers if you must!"

"I shall. Good night, Friend."

"Good night! I'll see thee the morrow. Right here. Let's make it nine o'clock."

Art watched as the prostitutes carried him off. Once he disappeared within, she turned and gazed up the Strand. She took ghost form and rose among the startled theater-goers. She willed herself to fly and flew fast.

She didn't bother with entering the lobby of the Secret Commission. She flew directly into its third floor and startled the clerks and accountants. She regretted the reckless display, but had intended to make that impression upon them. The theatric worked. Once she located the payer's booth, the pinched-faced clerk was unsettled and therefore willing to issue her further allowance. She took the money and flew to Whitechapel Market.

It required several queries and tireless flying, but she located each of the slaughter men she'd harmed earlier. The last one was lying in his bed dying. He was the one who had been flung to the rafters; in impacting them, his brain and organs had been damaged. Both his head and body were unnaturally swollen with fluids. Art paid the doctor to administer more morphine.

The slaughter man was no longer of right mind; with each breath he emitted a torturous moan. The children had been sent to stay across the street, but everyone living near could hear him. Art sat with his young wife and watched over him until he passed in the morning.

CHAPTER FOUR

Morning was muggy and gray. Art stood reading a newspaper amid the scattered litter in front of the closed Gaiety Theatre. Two young women dressed respectably as shop assistants approached. They carried Jim. Seeing him, Art folded her newspaper and smiled.

"Did Miss Skycourt cover the Hillings murder properly?" Jim greeted when he and the young women arrived.

"As if we saw same," Art said. She accepted Jim from the women. They bade him farewell and walked on. They were not the same women from last night, but it didn't surprise Art if these shop girls prostituted as well. There was only so much they could make working a legitimate position.

"How did you spend the night?" Jim asked. "If you were haunting a belfry, I'd suggest you try somewhere more fun next time."

"No Friend," she said. She set her stick to the walk and proceeded towards the West End. The shop girls were ahead of her. In solemn words she explained what happened to the slaughter man.

"I thought I saw the change in you," Jim said somberly. "I'm sorry."

"I've made my first mistake," she said.

"Your first accident, Art. It was an accident. Like running him over during a pursuit before realising it. Or scaring him into a shock that kills him. Or being unable to protect him during a battle because he was stupid or paralyzed with fear and in harm's way. We try our best, but things happen."

Art said nothing. She remembered how she threw the slaughter man, unknowing of her own strength, how he hit the rafters hard enough to bring horror to her heart.

"I will be caring for his widow, Fiona Bell," she finally said.

"Whatever you need to do to bear it," Jim said. "You can have the Commission pay recompense."

"I visited the payer this morning."

"Good. That's his blood on your front, isn't it?"

Art glanced down. She'd forgotten. No wonder the newsboy had stared in morbid awe at her bosom. Dennis Bell coughed in his agony, and blood came up. The family had no running water, so she left the stain as it was.

"All right," Jim said when she didn't answer. "As you suggested, we will replicate Mrs. Hillings' little shopping ritual. Off to Regent Street, then. You deserve your tea room time, anyway. My treat. Just make sure I've a pretty doily to sit on."

Liberty's tea room nearly refused them, and Art knew it was because she was less than presentable. Jim used the privilege of being agents to garner them a window table finally.

"I may look a beggar woman soon," Art said when she had taken her seat. Jim was placed on a fine doily across from her as requested.

"No! The blood stain only adds to your otherworldly charm! You may make a wreck of that finery yet and become the perfect ragged spectre of vengeance. But! Your hat will remain both coquettish and dashing. Now, let's act inconspicuous and almost human so we can hear what the silly birds twitter about."

Art smiled. She attempted to eavesdrop while enjoying the

sight of fine linen, china, and silverware. She was served tea, cakes, and other delicacies. She found she could not eat one tart, cake, biscuit, scone, or sandwich no matter how desirable they looked, though at Jim's urging she nibbled. She gazed at the curd and jams wistfully. When berries and cream were provided and the untouched plates of cakes and sandwiches removed by the server, she absorbed the berries as discreetly as she could into her body. The cream was left on the plate.

"Good to see you're at least making a pretense of enjoying that tea. When you raise the cup it makes you look the picture of a most noble and fine lady and less an undead creature."

"I am drinking, Friend, it appears I can. The scent and taste is pleasing."

"Drink and you may have to relieve yourself later. I hated that about Billy, always having to take a piss. God, I could eat a cigarette. Well, I've overheard something finally, how about you?"

"I listened to the women at several tables, though each time their words only reflect the papers."

"Isn't it nice that Fall gifts us agents with more powerful senses. I could do without the superior nose sometimes," Jim commented.

"I merely stop breathing."

"Doesn't work for me. Well, you chose the wrong gossips to focus on. The birds over there—that one in hideous blue and the other with the boat of a hat—have just had a patronizing conversation concerning our late Mrs. Hillings. Seems she had several children besides the littler one; three previous girls. I remember their portraits on the parlour mantle. Unfortunately, they're all dead."

"Illness?"

"Isn't that always the case," Jim said. "Excellent motivation for wanting the three-year-old babe back."

"The room is filled now," Art observed. "Perhaps this is the usual time for Mrs. Hillings to be here. I believe I see the answer she needed."

"Really? What's that?"

Outside the tea room window, an old bearded sandwichman wearing his brightly illustrated boards had arrived and was slowly pacing to and fro. He was advertising a medium and mesmerist who talked to the dead. Art told Jim what she saw.

"Madame Chance," she added.

"Art, mediums are a dime a dozen in this city," Jim said. "What makes you think our unfortunate Mrs. Hillings went to this particular one?"

Dime, Art thought. She knew what that was: an American coin. She reached over, picked Jim up, and showed him the sandwichman. The beautiful medium with her knowing eyes was painted embracing angelic ghost children to her. Her place of business was a short walk away.

"That's worth a doily sitting," Jim said.

～

On the street, Art set her stick for the direction of Madame Chance's address and walked among the lady window shoppers and young affluent girls seeking luncheon. A bobby glared at Art until he saw her badge.

"Before you're taken for a beggar woman you'll be mistaken for a prostitute first," Jim said.

"'Tis expected," Art murmured.

"Male pests are not deterred by blood stains or rags. Or even by your badge. This area is notorious, thanks to the explosion of women shoppers. That bold fellow there, top hat and looking the banker. That's right, look forward! Jerk," Jim said.

Art paused in step, trying to fathom Jim's use of the word "jerk."

"It's a good thing you've a man in your hand, Art, you're getting less harassment," Jim said self-importantly.

"Thee is my most chivalrous defender," Art said. "And cunning of tongue."

"Did you say what I thought you just said," Jim said in mirth.

"Aye." Art smiled. "I remember some things. But some words that thee says I've no recollection or understanding."

Jim glowered in her hand. Art observed his mood change with surprise and waited.

"Did that Fall say something!" Jim finally ejected. "He had my partners spy on me! Harold refused to write things down, but Deck was idiot enough to obey! God, I hated it! Everything that fell out of my teeth, questioned and duly recorded!"

"I've neither pen nor paper," Art said. "I only note that thee is inventive in speech, in manner beyond my ken."

"Well, I'd call it evidence you weren't much for society. Quakers aren't up on the latest fashionable phrases. I mean, who's speaking strangely here? I'm not the one thee-ing."

"Friend," Art said patiently.

"Or you're just not well read," Jim said.

"I read perfectly well," Art said with mild severity. "Cast no stones."

"All right, all right!" Jim said. He hopped in her hand. "I do speak queerly! It's just stuff that comes out of my head! Maybe I was a poet. Or a touched minister. And no, don't ask me what I mean when I say my *bon mots*. I get confused too."

"No harm," Art said gently. "'Tis queer speech, simply."

"I may be American," Jim said.

Art placed her walking stick on her arm and straightened his top hat.

"My weighty Friend," she said with a smile.

"I'm not so heavy as that!" Jim said.

"I meant thee is my wise friend. 'Tis Quaker."

"Now who's speaking queerly," Jim said, but his tone was warm. They presently stood before the building in which Madame Chance resided.

"Ladies first," Jim said chivalrously.

Art entered the foyer of the building and found Madame Chance's name on the wall directory. She walked into the lobby only to find a vertical tube containing an ornate gated cage.

"How fashionable! They've an ascending cage," Jim exclaimed. "Take us in!"

Art warily poked it with her stick.

"I prefer the stairs," she said.

"It's not going to eat us!" Jim said. "You were perfectly fine with the Commission's ascending room. Get in!"

Art opened the cage, entered, closed the gate, and set the lever. As the gears grinded and the cage slowly ascended she stood stiffly. The cage's bars surrounded her. She found she had a deep dislike of them.

The cage stopped at the fourth floor. Art left it as quickly as possible. The apartment they sought was at the end of the hall. She rapped on the door with her stick and Madame's assistant, a slightly built and haughty man, answered. He let them into the spacious apartment, but upon realising they had no appointment refused their request to see the medium.

"Madame is presently with a group," the man said. Though his air was snobbish, he was nervous before Art. "But you may make an appointment and request one of her services."

"We've no need of her services, man, we're already dead and know it!" Jim said. "She behind that door? What's going on in there?"

"Now, sir!" The assistant hurried to block their way as Art approached the door. "You mustn't go in. It's a very serious, sensitive ritual she's leading—"

Art reached around the man and turned the doorknob. The door opened upon a darkened room. She tossed Jim over the assistant's head and passed through the man in ghost form. The assistant screamed in fright.

In the dark room sat well dressed men around a table,

holding hands. At the head of the table a beautiful woman with her long hair down was seated, dressed only in a loosened dressing gown. Her breasts showed. She held hands with the men on either side of her. A lone candle on the table flickered. Art and Jim had interrupted a séance. The men gaped at the sight of Art.

"Gentlemen!" Jim said. "Your orgiastic summons has succeeded. Ghost and Skull are now here. But we're not in the mood to do any bidding. We could eat a soul, though. Who's ready to offer theirs?"

The men rose hastily and ran for the door.

"But Ghost is hungry, gentlemen!" Jim protested. Once the men retrieved their hats, sticks, and overcoats they were gone. Art silently closed the door on the gaping assistant.

"Madame Chance. As a medium you're probably aware of who we are. Lovely lack of ensemble you're wearing. Nice digs, too," Jim said. Art took his strange phrase as her cue to direct Jim about the room so he could take it in. Having superior eyesight the dark did not bother them. The place was wallpapered and hung with thick red drapes. Art suspected they concealed more than the walls behind them, as per the tricks of a pretender who supposedly summoned spirits and apparitions.

When Art returned her and Jim's attention to the medium, the woman was weighing Jim with a distant gaze. Chance lifted her chin in mild disdain.

"You're not supposed to be here at all," she said coolly. She turned to Art. Whatever she saw in Art immediately made Chance smile. The curl to her rouged lips was rueful.

Scantily clothed and smaller than Art, Chance had a confidence and presence that overpowered the room. She did not bother closing her gown but placed her hands on her hips, displaying her body further. Art was aware of the woman's distinct scent and bared skin, luminous and slightly flushed. The color of her hair matched that between her thighs. Despite the

distraction of the provocative display, Art was heedful of a bodi-
ly pulsation, subtle and steady, that Chance exuded. Art could
not see it, but if she reached out she thought she might touch
the tangible proof of a powerful aura.

"I see you find my partner interesting," Jim said. "But you
know who else we find interesting, Madame? A woman named
Mrs. Hillings."

"Mrs. Harriet Hillings?" Chance said, staring at Art.

"That's the one. And what business did she have with you?"

"I helped her see her child, two days ago," Chance said softly.

"Indeed? Which child? Since she had five," Jim asked.

"Why, the littlest girl. Just at that precious age where you
think she might make it. Might reach five," Chance whispered
to Art.

"You sound as if you've known this to happen. Child death,"
Jim said.

"I've helped many women see their children. It's what I do,"
Chance said.

"And help them rise again?" Jim asked, weight in his tone.

"What an odd and terrible question. To snatch the soul from
rest," Chance answered. She laid a hand on Art's chest where
the bloodstain lay. It was the same spot as Art's heart.

"Dear, you needn't look a spectre," Chance said, amused.
"You've women to care for."

Art chose not to react to the mysterious comment, though it
surprised her. Was Chance speaking of Fiona Bell?

"But that's what's happening, Madame," Jim said. "Things
have been raised. Things that shouldn't."

"Like yourself?" Chance said derisively, briefly acknowledging him. She returned her attention to Art. "Those creatures
haven't souls. Not like you."

"Then you know," Jim said. "You know about the re-animations."

"I have seen the future," Chance said to Art. "I know what

our sex will become in a hundred years' time. Everything about us will change."

"Women shall prance naked?" Jim said. "Callooh callay! I look forward to it. By the way, my compliments on such a crass distraction technique for 'mesmerizing' your clients. Makes it easier to pull your parlour tricks, doesn't it?"

"Baring my skin is a means of feeling for the presence of spirits," Chance said to Art. "And making intimate contact with them." She smiled, her hands touching her own shoulders. Her gown opened further. "I'm sure my communication technique has worked for you."

Art smiled and said nothing.

"I'm done with your questions," Chance then announced. "And you've lost me income. It's time for you to leave."

Jim surprisingly stayed silent, and though Chance did not touch her, Art felt she was being pushed out the door. She turned reluctantly, wondering how their visit had gone so awry. Before she exited Art felt compelled to glance back. Chance's gaze seemed to swallow her.

"Yours will be legend," Chance said. "And come to you again."

The assistant quickly showed them out. With Madame's apartment door firmly closed behind them, Art stood in the hallway in confusion.

"Well, we botched that," Jim declared.

"I was most politely given an eldering," Art said.

"Indeed. And bestowed enigmatic gifts as well. But for what?"

"I know not," Art said.

"Aren't you glad she's not your mother?" Jim said drily. "No more blood stains for you, young lady."

As Art moved for the ascending cage, Jim noticed the building across, seen through a hall window.

"That has a substantial ledge. Think you can jump to it?" he asked.

Happy to avoid another cage ride, Art climbed out the window with Jim and did. Once across, Art followed the ledge for a discreet view of the street below and the exit from Madame Chance's building. She stood before a large advertisement board of a smiling woman performer on a swing.

"Perhaps Madame will go visit Mr. Devilish," Jim said. "Or, vise-versa."

Art stood still and patiently against the board while they watched. They attracted no attention except from pigeons.

"I rather like Lulu Wren," Jim said, having twisted in Art's hand to admire the advertisement.

"Friend, thee spoke of how I must learn to discern who had real power and who had none," Art said. "I felt that Chance is not a charlatan."

"Yes," Jim sighed. "She's real. Too bad her sort speaks riddles. And in case she was more witch than spiritualist, I made sure not to give our names—you know. So she could name us. When I insulted her craft I was trying to goad her, make her say something helpful. However, it seemed she more turned your head. You were entirely distracted, Art."

"She is a sensual woman," Art said.

"Pungent," Jim said. "Stags would've come a runnin'. I prefer my women less maenad. Huh, sensual? You're a woman, you know what one looks like. Or are you trying to tell me something?"

"I am. I may have love of women," Art said.

"Oh HO HO HO!" Jim laughed. "HO! Not only were you a criminal, but a pervert!"

"God loves," Art said firmly. "I love. 'Tis that which matters."

"Heh heh. You call it love. Good luck with that. But you're in good company. Harold liked the gents a little too much, and Molly—hm, you'll probably end up meeting her, but best keep you two apart. You seem so sexless, Art. Not that pneumatic body of yours, but your mind. Did you only realise it now?"

"No," Art said. She recalled Helia's blue eyes. "And I hadn't time for sweethearting, Friend."

Jim chuckled dolefully. "We never do," he said.

They saw a woman emerge from the building. She was not Madame Chance. Art relaxed.

"My head may have been turned, but I noticed one thing," Art said.

"What, that she had two breasts as well as two eyes? She didn't grace us with her back, but I assure you, she had two buttocks."

Art glanced at Jim askance and he chuckled.

"She had a wallpaper. 'Twas a theme," Art said. "The image same upon her gown. 'Twas the Tree of Life."

"I saw the paper, didn't see her gown," Jim said. "Ar! High magic users! 'Just helps women see their children,' my eye sockets. Well, that does it. Madame is complicit. I hope she puts clothes on and does something soon. We may be here a while."

"Friend, as long as she's unclothed, she may be entirely aware that we are still here."

"That's true. So much for subterfuge. Think lustful thoughts about her, Art, maybe that will force her out," Jim said.

"I haven't love of her that much," Art muttered.

Her badge abruptly glowed.

"Ulp! Buzz buzz! And what a message," Jim said. Art saw that Jim's pin, stored in his skull, caused his eye sockets to glow.

"How do I receive the same?" Art asked.

"Tap you badge, it will be a speaking telegraph." She did and a voice spoke from the badge.

"Killing at Beauchamp Dress Salon." The voice was male, his intonation loud and clear, as if he were present with them. "Re-animation sighted. Address is as follows."

Art listened in surprise as the voice gave an address with the names of its nearest streets.

"Art, tap your badge again before that's repeated," Jim said. "Hate these vocalized messages, that's why I usually take the communiqué. It sounds in my head, not aloud like that. Imagine that happening when one is meant to be discreet, like right now."

"Can he hear us?" Art said.

"No, it's one-way. We end it, he knows we received it. Let's go before the corpse gets stiffer."

~

The salon was near. Its ornate doors opened when Art stepped upon the illustrated gold mat within the portico. As she entered, bejeweled mechanical birds musically greeted her from silver trees on each side. Art walked beyond the trees only to be startled at the sight of herself and Jim reflected in large gold mirrors hung on the walls. One was cracked from impact, blood sprayed upon it. Dress models huddled at one end of the showroom while two bobbies hovered over the body beneath the mirror. Blood was smeared all around the woman, fresh and red.

"How long ago did this happen?" Jim demanded when they neared the body. "And who is she?"

"Not fifteen minutes, sir," one of the bobbies answered quickly. "It's the proprietress, Madame Beauchamp, sir." The older woman was torn open, the iridescent fabric of her dress glistening blood.

Jim called to the women at the other side of the showroom. "Who saw this happen? Who did it? Give us a name, a description!"

"It—it was the fabric runner, sir! Just this little boy we used," a woman shakily said. Unlike the models wearing colourful gowns with bows and ribbons, the woman was plainly dressed in black.

"And you are?" Jim asked.

"Madame's assistant, sir. I was right by her when the boy came in. He ran straight for her, sir. And then he was killing her. It was horrible."

"What's more horrible is that he's supposed to be dead!" one of the models cried. "He died only days ago, hit by a cab while running fabric to the dressmaker!"

"Which dressmaker? Where is it? And who's the boy's mother?" Jim demanded.

"Why, she works there, sir," the assistant said. "She works at the shop, it's in the East End."

Art quickly spun; she felt an eldritch signal, flashing somewhere far like a gaslight erupting.

"Send Inspector Risk to the sweatshop and make sure he knows where NOW!" Jim cried as Art ran out the doors.

She sped down the crowded thoroughfare filled with omnibuses, carts, and cabs. She pushed through pedestrians. She saw a portly cabman frantically whipping the air, a ragged boy upon him. The cabman fell off his seat and into the street.

When Art reached the frightened cab horses, passers-by were trying to hold the animals. A thick crowd gathered around the cabman's body. He stared sightlessly up, his throat and chest torn, his intestines pulled out. Art shoved through the crowd and ran again.

"He's not killed his last, I'm sure of it!" Jim cried. "Faster Art, faster!"

Art was quick, but the boy was smaller and swifter. When she couldn't keep him in sight, she probed for his eldritch signal. It burned like a small, malevolent fire rushing to one purpose. The boy ran wildly down the congested thoroughfares for the twisted streets of the East End. More carts packed high with furniture and goods blocked Art's path. She leapt and ran across the tops, recklessly close to slipping. She hit the ground only to be struck by a costerman's cart that rapidly rolled into her. As she stumbled she saw the boy run into a tenement building.

"Damn it!" Jim shouted. "You should have left me at the salon!"

"Too late!" Art said. "Stand by me Friend, for I'll need thee! I must kill the child," she said desperately. She ran for the building and up the stairs.

Screams came from the garret. Art burst into the sweatshop full of frightened women in time to see the boy attack the head dressmaker, clinging to her struggling body while his gory hands ripped at her chest. Fleeing seamstresses fell and tripped Art, nearly sending her head into a rafter. She tossed Jim to the fabric-covered table and leapt for the boy, grabbing him by the neck. She yanked him off the woman. He lunged in her grasp and bit down hard on her other arm. She pulled him away. Her flesh tore and she saw her own blood, strange and pale, fly in the air. The meat of her flesh was also pale. The boy twisted and chomped down on the arm that had him and she flung him off. His small body crashed through the window. She jumped through the jagged hole for the street below.

"ART, YOUR MONOCLE!" she heard Jim cry.

She landed on the street feet first but the boy was already up and madly running, his broken arm flailing. She retrieved her monocle and took ghost form.

⁓

In the sweatshop, Jim spat out his pin.

"Who knows what this is?" Jim cried. "First smart girl to accept it must help me, and hurry!"

A girl hurried forward. She followed Jim's directions. She found his monocle and placed it at his eye socket, retrieved his brown candle, and lit it.

"That boy's mother!" he said to the frightened women. "Where is she?"

The seamstresses moved aside. A woman sat slumped among the scattered, half-made dresses, keening softly. Her eyes were wide with grief and horror.

"Never mind," Jim said. He turned his attention to his

monocle. Art was rapidly ghosting through advertisement boards, omnibuses, fences, horses, carts, and crowds of people. The undead boy ran just beneath her. She was flying.

"That's it!" Jim said. "He'll lead us to the re-animationist!"

"Aye," Art whispered in his skull. She was so close to her quarry Jim could see the grimy wheel track across the boy's dirty shirt back.

Art shadowed the undead boy as he leapt fences and scurried thorough laundry-hung warrens, ran through yards scattering chickens, and barreled through back kitchens, frightening people with his bloodstained body. When the boy ran into a deserted street that led into a decrepit tenement, Art took solid form. He disappeared inside. The area was silent and lifeless. Art stood on the cobblestones and felt the black presence that shifted and flickered within the building.

"Street name, Art, I need a sign," Jim said in her ear. Art slowly pivoted around to view the empty street until she faced the tenement again.

"I have it," Jim said. "What's wrong?"

"They're all here," she quietly said.

"Don't go in," Jim said. "Wait for us. I hear Risk on the stairs now."

"No. Thee saw what the little one can do. More men will die if I don't enter."

"I understand. I—" He fumbled for words. "Art," he said.

"Yes," she said. "I'll do it."

"We'll be there as fast as we can." He fell silent.

She walked towards the building. Above, the tiny shadows waited. She grasped her stick in both hands.

"Way will open," Art whispered. She stilled the tremor of her hands.

In ghost form she passed through all the floors. At the topmost one she rose in the presence of still and silent children. She took solid form in the midst of them.

The re-animationist stood across the room, leaning against a wall. The undead boy with the broken arm clung to him. The children stood pale and dead-eyed. Some had rotting wounds. A boy's neck had the thick purplish bruises from being garroted. A little girl in a fine white dress was cut open from her neck down to her legs. The littlest child among them was a tiny girl of three.

"Surprised to see so many?" the man asked. He was darkly handsome but his face was wan and perspiring. He leaned heavily against the wall.

"The parent who loves would want them back," Art said.

"Yes," the man agreed. "They need to come back; especially if they were murdered."

"And it's not an accident," he continued when Art did not respond. "If the intention was clear. The dead know. YOU should know."

Art remained silent. She was counting the children.

"I had a daughter," the man said. "That's how it began. But the raising is not easy. There has to be a reason; a strong and compelling reason. That reason is revenge."

"Thee looks unwell, Friend," Art softly said.

The man took a breath. "It's an effort. . . keeping them still. Though they've all made those pay who should. Perhaps it's time."

He gazed wild-eyed at Art.

"I know you'll take care of it," he said. "CHILDREN, EAT THE GHOST!"

The man ran. The undead set upon Art like rabid dogs. Her stick came down and crushed the littlest girl's head. She smashed two of the children together and their heads popped like melons. She threw down the ones who bit her and raised her boot to crush them. She didn't want a single one to leave that room.

It was short work. But for Art the killing seemed endless until she finally realised she swung at nothing. Only she remained standing. She forced her feet to step over the small, maimed bodies and left.

As she stumbled for sunlight, her torn dress trailed, leaving a smear of old black blood and gore. Her own blood ran in pale rivulets through the stains and rips. Small hands had clawed across her breast and her back, shredding her to the skin. More bites had been taken out of her arms. The fingers of her left hand did not respond; she wondered if she still had any. Her face hurt.

Horse-drawn wagons thundered into the street and were brought around, the policemen in the wagons clinging to the sides. A penny-farthing sped after them, and Helia Skycourt jumped off at a run, laying her wheel quickly down. Dozens of policemen disembarked and ran for the building. Risk leapt out of a hackney carriage with Jim in hand.

"Top floor, I think she got all of them, but be careful lest one got away!" Jim cried as Risk ran past Art. "And the man's on the run, so spread your men!"

"All right men!" Risk shouted. "Come around! Look at this drawing, here's your man!"

Art heard more orders given and the men organized themselves. There was the trampling of feet and then strangely, silence. She noticed the handle of her walking stick. It was sticky with brain and hair. She tipped it down and awkwardly rubbed the handle end against her skirts. A shadow fell upon her. Art raised her head to see.

Helia stood near. In her wide eyes Art saw no fear or grief, no maudlin sympathy. Helia's stark gaze held a deep well that spoke of shared pain, of knowledge and understanding.

"Dost thee know me?" Art whispered.

Helia softened; her eyes grew bright.

"I do," Helia said. She stepped closer. She pulled a white handkerchief from her sleeve and gently placed it at Art's face where she bled.

Forget-me-not, Art thought.

Art raised her left hand for the one against her face. Hers shook. She remembered that she might be missing fingers.

"I've dirtied thy glove," Art softly said.

Helia blinked and her lips parted in a strange smile. She turned her hand with the handkerchief to look at it.

"They know blood," Helia said. Her smile faded.

"What do you need?" she then gently asked.

"Raw food," Art whispered.

"Animal?"

"Aye."

"Hooved or bird?"

"No."

"Wait here," Helia bade. She stepped back. "Wait here, wait here, wait here." She turned and ran.

Art stood on the walk and waited. That was what Helia had said to do.

She raised her head when she heard the fast trundle of cart wheels. Helia ran beside a costerman pushing his barrow full of eels.

"For you," Helia said breathlessly once the cart stopped before Art. Her eyes shined brightly and her cheek was flushed. "Oh please, eat."

Art raised her stick towards the eels. They were alive and twitching. She drew them towards her and they flew, glistening and thrashing into her body. Their tails whipped before disappearing inside of her. Art jerked from their wiggling. As she digested the eels her wounds closed, her bitten fingers cracked into place, and her pains fled. Her body fiercely glowed. Helia pressed both her gloved hands to her mouth in delight. She danced. The costerman fell down, trembling.

Art's glow diminished. She raised her left hand. The glove was covered in black blood and gore but all fingers were present. She fumbled for the badge at her breast. Helia's hand stopped hers.

"I paid," she said, smiling.

A policeman ran up to them, holding Jim. When he reached Art's side Helia let go. Art held her hand out for Jim. The policeman balked at seeing the state of Art's gloved fingers, but placed Jim in them.

"Art, I'm sorry," Jim said. "They ran off with me and well, spirit of the chase and all. Thank God you ate, you're looking better."

"They captured him?" Art asked.

"Not yet," Jim said. "Lady Skycourt! I'm Jim Dastard. If I may be so bold as to address you. Not every pretty woman wears such a distinct mask. Shouldn't you join the other journalists gaining entrance to the re-animationist's lair? All his reanimations are dead again, thanks to Art. This stalwart bobby will accompany you."

Helia looked at Art. The policeman waited. Helia removed her notebook and pencil from her dress pockets.

"Yes," she agreed. "Yes, let's look at them." She followed the policeman.

"Did she bother you too much, Art?" Jim asked when Helia entered the building. "These journalists can be aggressive. She didn't upset you, did she?"

"No, Friend," Art said.

"Let's leave. Risk has this completely in hand, and we've done our part. Keep going down this way. You need to clean up and refresh. Yes, fast tracks!"

Art's stick hit the walk as she moved down the street. "This spectre nonsense doesn't suit you," Jim said. "I want my queenly Clydesdale back. There's a very nice establishment nearby, a prince of a place. They'll take very good care of us and especially of you. Just keep walking, I'll tell you when."

"I am a spectre. 'Tis fitting," Art said, her voice distant.

"No. Not for you. We may embrace who we are now, these extraordinary creatures, but not to the detriment of our souls. We are the evidence, Art, of what true resurrection is. We are not demons, and I won't let you look like one. Keep going, not long now."

Art turned her head to look behind her. Helia had eluded her policeman. She trailed several feet behind Art on her penny-farthing, her foot on the treadle. Helia smiled and waved.

"Art, turn down here. We're going to enter a club. A hoity-toity one, but very discreet."

Art saw the secluded entrance deep within an intimate portico. A round iris door gleamed within; it was the typical secured entrance of exclusive gentlemen's clubs, fashionably mimicking the spiral hatches of airships. Art turned to Jim.

"What manner of place is this?" she asked. "And between the impoverished places?"

"Art, it's a club. You'll like it, because I like it, and I believe I know what you like! Now let's get you inside. Your wounds are no longer dripping, but you are a fright."

"'Tis a brothel," Art said flatly.

"It's not a—look, it's just like the gent clubs. Grooming, meals, relaxation, a place to sleep. Very civilized. The only difference is there's women present. That's the place's charm. It's run by women and they do the caring. I'm a member, Art, it's most respectable."

"Thee should say it, 'tis made for sex," Art said.

"It's not a brothel! 'Tis made for trysts or treats. Now get in, Art!"

Art moved for the portico but glanced back again. Helia stood by her wheel, watching her unabashedly. A delighted smile was on her lips. Helia motioned for Art to enter and winked.

CHAPTER FIVE

When Art stood before the iris door, Jim produced a key stamped "VESTA" from between his teeth. She inserted it in the panel next to the door and turned it. The metal blades of the iris spiraled open, and Art stepped into the club's foyer. It was manned by a pair of uniformed footmen, dressed in breeches and stockings.

As the iris spun shut behind her, Art noticed that the footman nearest her was not a man but a tall, lean woman with handsome features. Art stared at her. The woman, in turn, froze at the grisly sight of Art.

"How is the Spirit with thee, Friend?" Art finally greeted.

"Doris, just help the Quaker in," Jim said to the shocked footwoman.

The other footwoman who matched Doris in height and build responded more quickly. She fetched floor covering used for bad weather and quickly rolled it out. Art stepped upon it. Both women worked rapidly to cover the fine carpeting of the foyer and hallway until Art arrived at the main staircase. A boyish-faced young woman liveried as a page came to join her. During her slow and steady passage into the club, Art noticed the rooms of the main floor: the library, the card room, the curiousities and mechanical room, two drawing rooms on each side of the hall, and a billiards room. The different drawing rooms drew Art's attention. One held men, some flamboyantly dressed, while the other had women. A few of the women were dressed in various styles of men's attire, complete with men's shoes and watch chains. Some were in full gentlemen's evening dress. Occupants from both drawing rooms stepped out to stare at Art.

"If you'll follow me, Miss," the page said while Art returned the gentry's stares.

"Lead on, Alice," Jim said.

Bemused, Art followed Alice up the stairs.

On the third floor, Art was shown a spacious room with a large bed. The deep red colour of the wallpaper, carpet, curtains, pillows, and bedding reminded Art of Madame Chance. Maids were already inside pulling down a porcelain tub stored in a closet. They rolled the tub into the center of the room and began filling it with buckets of hot water.

"Welcome to the Vesta Club, Miss," Alice said to her.

"Art, go in," Jim said encouragingly. "Yes, it's very refined, but not so refined for a Quaker."

Once inside, Alice relieved Art of Jim and the maids moved forward to undress her. One maid struggled to take the walking stick from Art's hand until Art remembered to release it. Her hat and soiled gloves were removed, her bodice pulled off, then her skirt unhooked. Her under-bodice, underskirt, and petticoats came off next. Though Alice stood discreetly aside with Jim, her eyes grew large from staring at Art's arms and shoulders.

"Oh my!" the maid behind Art said once the corset was undone. "Bitten through—"

"Hush," the maid in front of Art said. "Let's get this off." She placed her hands around Art's waist to do so and removed the corset.

Something pitter pattered on the carpet floor. It was a child's tooth.

Art stayed the second maid's hands so she could look at the corset. Teeth marks were clearly visible on the bone and plating. One of the metal bones was pulled away by a bloody mouth that had refused to let go.

"Almost done, Miss," the maid said, gently taking the corset from Art's fingers. She looked up at Art and smiled. "Boots and stockings and everything else, soon."

"Art, I have to step out for a moment!" Jim suddenly exclaimed. "Carry on, I'll be right back!" Alice walked Jim out of the room.

Finally Art was nude and ushered into the bath. The first maid picked up Art's boots; the soles were caked with gore and matted blond hair. The second maid calmly rolled Art's soiled and sticky dress into a bundle with the undergarments. The front of her white apron was stained from the black blood. She picked up the corset and dented metal bustle. She showed none of the queasiness of her companion, who was gingerly holding Art's boots. Art raised her arm from the tub and touched the second maid. The woman glanced at her in surprise, and then smiled.

"Miss, I helped nurse in Kabul during the second Afghan war," she said. "You're a warrior, aren't you? It's no different."

The maid rose. As the two women exited, Art gazed at the bundle being carried out and realised that bits of children were in it.

She sat in the hot tub and watched the steam rise. She strangely felt no warmth.

There was a knock and a large, pleasant-faced woman appeared, carrying two buckets of hot water and a stool. She ambled over to the tub and set the stool behind Art.

"Oh, now that's a fine head of hair!" she exclaimed, removing the pins. Art's hair fell, long and thick. "Let's give it a good wash!"

Art tilted her head back when ordered and felt the soothing rush of water poured through her tresses. She wondered how much blood had gotten into it.

There was another knock, and after a moment's pause the door opened. A well-dressed older woman stepped in, her demeanor pensive. Her face did not show much age, but her dark hair was already streaked with white. Alice, carrying Jim, followed her. The woman walked around the tub, and Art determined that she wasn't the housekeeper. She wore one fine jewel on her dark bodice, the sapphire sparkling at her breast.

"I'm Mrs. Catherine Moore. Owner of the Vesta Club," the woman said solemnly. "I'll be so presumptuous as to speak for my recently deceased friend, Madame Beauchamp, and thank you for defending her and others who would have also met horrible ends if not for your aid."

Art looked at her in confusion.

"The dress salon owner, Art," Jim reminded her.

"Alice, a chair," Mrs. Moore demanded. Alice quickly fetched one and set it before the tub. Mrs. Moore sat down facing Art.

"My son Harold was like you, an agent of the Secret Commission. In the short time I had him back he accomplished wondrous acts of heroism. He was a more outstanding being as an agent than he was when he first lived. My husband and I could not be prouder. And I could only love him more." Catherine paused and she blinked. "You are invited to stay at the Vesta Club for as long as you wish," she then said. "It's the least we can do in appreciation of your service."

Catherine rose to leave.

Art spoke at last, her voice soft. "My thanks, Friend."

When Catherine left, Jim had Alice set him in the vacated chair. The woman behind Art finished washing her hair, picked up her buckets, and with a friendly farewell, left too. The door shut and Art and Jim were alone.

"How's that tub?" Jim asked.

Art felt the heat seep into her.

"Very good," she said. "This is an expensive place."

"We could never afford it on our salary," Jim said. "Her son Harold was my first partner. A good man. I toast him fondly. This has been my haven since, and I'm rather selfish about it. Since the partners I had after Howard all spied for Fall I never let them in here."

"My thanks for sharing it," Art said.

"I'm probably sharing it because you're a woman. And because I can get you to share expenses. We are staying here somewhat for free, but you can be certain the Vesta discreetly tallies everything else for the Secret Commission! Including, well. . . Art, let's talk about sex."

"My sex?" Art said.

"No, I don't mean about women. Or about men, though the men here are mandrakes. I mean sex. Sex. Sex!" Jim exclaimed.

Art put her sponge down and looked at him.

"Come now, don't be coy," Jim said. "You used the exact word with that exact meaning, outside. We must discuss this, Art."

"Friend, I prefer not," Art said.

"You're a sapphist, the club is full of sapphists, don't you want to talk 'plainly' and about lights and truths like Quakers are supposed to?"

"Aye, but I needn't know all truths," Art said.

"Oh, well I—Art! I wasn't talking about me! Let me at least mention it. Whether you feel it's sordid or natural. Animal or God-given. Or however you as a new kind of Quaker woman shall think of it—to dab, to dock, to knock, to roger—"

"I am learning new and most coarse terms of body," Art exclaimed.

"Oh good! Means you were an innocent before now. This is my advice." Jim said. "Have you a need: bill it."

"This is thy talk about sex," Art said slowly.

"Yes. Why, did you want to learn anything more?"

"'Tis enough. My thanks, Friend," Art quickly said.

"You are most welcome."

~

Her bath cooled. Art had the desire to finish with an invigorating cold splash. She wasn't sure why since it didn't sound appealing, but she might request such a cleansing next time. She liked the idea of a next time. She rose from the tub and stepped behind a folding screen hung with clean towels to dry her body. Carnality was embarrassing to discuss, but being nude in the presence of her partner did not bother her. Jim had seen her pole axed and set upon by ravenous undead children, nearly stripped and violated by predatory brothel workers. Nudity was a matter of trust.

"Friend, I am refreshed and recovered," Art said as she dried herself. "But my clothes are compromised. While I stay here, would thee like to return to Friend Risk and resume the chase?"

"It's a chase I must decline," Jim said. "It's Risk's hunt now. Good for our public relationship, you see. We're allowing Scotland Yard to take this one."

"Yet he is dealing with a mesmerist," Art said.

"True, but Risk has piled on the men. A fleeing warlock can only handle so many minds. Won't be long, it's a matter of manpower and time, and Risk is as tenacious as a bloodhound. Good God, Art, you're quite an accomplishment," Jim said.

He was referring to her body. Towel held around her, Art had left the screen to study herself in the room's full-length mirror. When she first awoke in the Secret Commission, she had been fully clothed, right down to hat and gloves. Seeing herself bare for the first time, she then understood the reactions she elicited whenever she was undressed. She was well-muscled but not so much like the typical, sturdy working woman capable of handling brawls and drunkard husbands. There was deliberate shape and definition to her musculature that satisfied her critical eye. She was surprised that she had such an eye.

She flexed an arm to study the result. Her bicep was of acceptable size and form.

"Absolutely artistic," Jim exclaimed behind her. "No question, you were a physical culturist. You rival Charmion! And I'm quite knowledgeable of my performers, from Zazel, the lovely Human Cannonball, to Blondin. If you had been a strongwoman, I would have seen you. Therefore, like a humble Quaker you probably lifted horses in obscurity."

"To exhibit myself would have gotten me above my Light," Art said.

"I disagree. There's no narcissism if that was never your intention. Craft and hard work is what I see in a woman shot out of a cannon, walking the rope, or flying through the air for the trapeze. They're sharing their gifts and bestowing upon us that one memorable moment full of awe and wonder. And a bit of fantasy indulgence, much to the male appreciation. I owe you a show. Have to get rid of more of that innocence."

Art smiled at him and moved her hair aside. She fixed her towel so that she could turn around and flex both arms. She critically regarded the definition of her back.

"'Tis good work, but needs more to be maintained," she said.

"Ho hum. Health enthusiasts. I forget that their passion for oats, ice-cold showers, and Grecian proportions makes me sleepy."

Art decided to not ask what "Grecian proportions" were. It sounded very learned, like university. What came to her mind were nude male statues with fig leaves. She flexed a leg to see the musculature. It appeared that as a body enthusiast she was well-rounded. She opened her towel to look at the whole of herself for symmetry. Then she noticed the white round scar over her heart.

She covered her breasts and went to Jim to show him the scar.

"That's from a bullet," he said. "And it killed you. Let's see your back." She turned around and dropped her towel further. "Yes. You were shot through. And by an excellent marksman."

"Yet I was hanged," Art said.

"You know that for certain?" Jim asked.

Art realised she didn't. There was a knock at the door. Alice returned with the maids. While the maids emptied the bath, Jim queried Alice about Art's clothes. Art stepped away and became aware of something. She stood apart from the activity to concentrate. She heard it again; a sound of movement behind the bedroom wall. When Art discerned steady, soft breathing she realised someone was peeping.

One of the maids stumbled while tilting the emptied bath back into its closet.

"Careful now!" Jim said.

When the maids and Alice left, Art returned her attention to the peeper. She sensed that person moving along the wall until that person departed too.

"You know, Art, you're too tall for borrowed clothes! Not to mention having a chest that could bump ships. All the women are of woman size next to you," Jim complained. "Even the men. They're summoning your dressmaker. Did you know your clothes were labeled down to the corset and bustle? Makes you quite the gay Quaker, eh?"

"Worldly dressed, aye. But likely I was plainly dressed, Friend, and made my own clothes. Before I was shot," Art said. "I know nothing of labels." She was about to poke her head into the wall in ghost form when there was another knock at the door.

"Art, can you get that please," Jim said. "My hands are full."

She opened the door.

Two young women stood in the hall, both of same height and build; one was dark-haired and one was blonde. Both had their hair down. A bald man with a waxed moustache stood a few feet behind them, his height rivaling Art's. He was thick-necked and well muscled. Art looked down at the women and saw the mischief in the pretty dark-haired woman's face. When she looked at the blonde woman Art saw. . .

Eyes. Large, heavy-lidded and green, lit with specks of brown, gray, and yellow, and which softly drew Art in by their encompassing stillness, solemnity, and curiosity. Art thought she breathed fresh air.

And though she was certain she'd never visited one, ancient woods came to the fore of her mind, powerful, majestic and alive.

"*Vous êtes déshabillée,*" the dark haired woman remarked.

Art shook her head. She broke her gaze with the blonde woman and tried to think.

"*Oui,*" Art finally said.

"*Je suis Arlette et elle est Manon,*" Arlette said, motioning to herself and her companion. Arlette had Art's newly polished boots in her hand. "*Le camarade derrière moi est Oleg! Nous avons apporté vos chaussures et d'autres articles de toilette. Pouvons-nous entrer?*"

Art stared at Arlette and realised that she really knew no French.

"Art, will you let those two in! Never mind Oleg, the big Russian behind them. He's their bully, and always waits outside."

Arlette gave Art her boots and entered. Manon followed more slowly and watched Art. Art closed the door. It was then she noticed that both women were barefoot.

"Silly girls, pretending to be servants!" Jim said as Arlette took his top hat off and kissed his forehead. "They perfectly well know how to speak English! Art, these beauties are the pride of Vesta! The dark one is Arlette and the lovely blonde is Manon. As you recall, I'm an enthusiast for entertainment, and theirs is of the most skilled and privileged sort. Arlette and Manon are, shall we say, sapphic performers."

"Such titles, monsieur!" Arlette said, playfully placing Jim's hat back on his skull. "Speak the truth!"

"I am!" Jim said. "You are two very, very, very talented women."

Arlette laughed.

Art remained silent, her head tilted pensively.

"Art. We've guests, this isn't time for Quaker thoughts," Jim said.

"Friend, I'm not having Quaker thoughts," Art said.

"Monsieur Dastard, one moment while I lay out toiletries for Art," Arlette said. She approached the dresser and unrolled a cloth. Inside were women's things: a hairbrush, hair pins, a bottle of lotion, a jar of cream, and other necessities. Arlette quickly arranged them on the dresser top.

"My thanks," Art said with quiet appreciation. She had come around the bed to the dresser and saw what was laid out. Such a simple gesture made her feel that she'd somehow become richer.

"Amenities does the soul good, doesn't it, Art?" Jim said. "Even Billy coveted his comb. I'm fond of a good toothbrush, myself."

"Is that a hint, monsieur?" Arlette asked lightly. "Shall I clean your teeth?"

"Oh my sweet, if you've the time, please do!" Jim said. Arlette picked him up and escorted him to the closet that contained the lavatory and basin stand.

Art still held her boots. They were scrubbed and polished a shiny black. She was about to place them on the floor when she noticed the silver caps that were tapped into the toes and in the back of each heel. She looked closely, having not had a chance to see her own shoes until then and finding the ornaments unconventional. The caps in back were inscribed with the words: ART.

Art balked. She glanced up when she became aware that Manon was slowly approaching. Art dropped her boots.

Manon walked carefully, toe first like a ballet dancer. She stared at Art with soft, focused scrutiny and then passed her. She stopped at the dresser and laid objects upon it. First were two keys, one stamped "VESTA" and the other a room key with a brass metal tag in the shape of a hearth. There was no room number, only the word "ROUGE." Then came Art's meager possessions: her Secret Commission badge, freshly polished, her monocle, also cleansed, her skull cameo, and her purse. The last object Manon laid down with solemnity was the silver engraved card of Helia Skycourt.

Manon turned to Art. "*Vous etes un fantome?*" she whispered.

Art wondered why she could understand her.

"Aye," she answered in a low voice.

"*Avez-vous vu ma soeur morte?*" Manon asked.

Have thee seen my dead sister, Art thought. During all her time ghosting Art had yet to see one spirit.

"I have seen none," Art said in a lost voice.

Anger swiftly entered Manon's eyes, and just as swiftly, tears. Art knelt before her, one hand held out. She felt she dared not touch Manon without permission.

"I am sorry," Art said. "That I am a ghost not allowed to see into heaven. Thee must know thy sister is one with love and Light, released from time and knowledge. May we rejoice in her next journey, proceeding as way opens."

She watched as Manon raised her chin. Manon slowly turned away, but as she did so she brushed her fingers in Art's open hand. Art felt something stir in her palm, like fresh earth broken by a seedling.

Jim and Arlette had returned from the wash basin and were watching them. Arlette placed Jim on the table by the curtained windows and held out her hand for Manon. They moved to leave and Arlette regarded Art.

"Welcome to the Vesta, Art. We will see you soon," she said with a smile. She closed the door behind them.

Art still knelt on the carpet. She wondered what had just happened.

"Art, you did a most un-Quaker thing," Jim said.

"What is that, Friend?" Art said, slowly rising.

"You bent your knee to Manon. You never curtsy, you never bow, you've not removed your hat anywhere, and you don't even nod. You won't even address Risk by his title, and he's just an inspector. I know you'd rather endure a head chopping than acknowledge Her Majesty as your sovereign, but you knelt for Manon."

"I did, for she is younger and I'll not stand above when speaking of her sister," Art said.

"You think you're that much older than her?" Jim asked in humour.

"Perhaps. 'Tis hard to tell with my height; we Clydesdales mature early in our proportions."

Jim laughed. "You'll never forgive me for calling you that."

Art smiled. "I'll not forgive thee for calling me Queen."

Jim chuckled and Art touched the bed's ornate pillows. She beheld her surroundings: the gaslight fixtures, wood furnishings, and thick drapes. She didn't think she'd known such fine things before.

"Oh, those who see us all equal, and only God worthy of veneration," Jim finally said. "But the Commission and I have got the plainness out of you! You're noticing, aren't you? Fine digs, fine clothes, fine sea crawly wallies to eat! Promise to never wear one of those awful bonnets, and I'll tolerate some of your charitable pursuits with orphans, orphaned widows, and orphaned animals and such."

Art's smile at Jim's words faded at the mention of orphans.

"When I was with the re-animationist—did thee follow our conversation?" she abruptly asked.

"Hm?" Jim said. "No. But I saw it. I was candle-less by then."

"He spoke of revenge," Art said. "Which gave purpose to the raising. All the children had been murdered."

"'Murder' seems broad a term here," Jim said thoughtfully. "Like our fabric runner. We know how abusive those salons are. Wretched girls have died in garrets sewing for them. Therefore, did the salon owner and the sweatshop dressmaker force an exhausted child to deliver fabric one too many times? Possibly. Though one would think he would blame his poor mother. And the driver? Did he run the boy down on purpose? Perhaps. It doesn't explain Mrs. Hillings's littlest girl. She killed her mother, who desperately wanted her back, and her baby brother."

"There were sixteen children," Art whispered.

"That's a significant amount of vengeful killing," Jim said. "But if many of those reanimations were children of the poor. . . or orphans, then the ones they killed in possible revenge would have not caught the attention of police or press. You'll notice that the newspapers only started reporting deaths when the victims turned up respectable."

Jim's eye sockets suddenly glowed.

"I'll take it," he said. He listened for a while as Art waited patiently. "Well, it's done."

"Friend?" Art asked.

"They had him cornered and he wearied, I bet," Jim said. "Our warlock had the policemen fight each other and then tried to run for it. Like I said, he couldn't influence the whole lot, and some gave chase. He fell to his death. Tried for a jump between buildings and lost."

"Friend, I forgot about Chance. What of her?" Art asked.

"Ah. I did remember her. When I stepped out I had a message sent to Risk. I'm sure he'll have her taken in. Well, my young friend! Excellent work. You'll probably celebrate the successful closing of your first case with thoughtful reflection or acts of charitable indulgence. Just don't try to rescue any of the residents of the Vesta. Manon and Arlette happen to be available, and I like to take advantage of their valuable company any chance I can get. Can you pull the cord over there? Alice will come and fetch me."

Alice came and picked up Jim. She let Art know that her clothes would soon be ready for mending. Her dressmaker was on her way.

"Finally you can regain your respectability!" Jim said. "Well, I'm off to lose mine. Be well my friend, and have a good night!"

"Good night, Friend," Art said.

As Jim left with Alice, a maid arrived through the doors with an armload of Art's clothes, smelling freshly steamed. In her hand was Art's newly polished walking stick; the deer's silver head gleamed. A small, thin red haired woman pushed her way past Alice and followed the maid in. She came up short at the sight of Art, recovered, and then briskly dropped off a brightly patterned carpet bag and a black folio tied shut with black string on the bedspread. The maid laid out Art's clothes on the bed while the woman pulled off her hat and gloves.

"I'm Charlotte Thackery, your dressmaker," Charlotte said. "I usually do not come to people's homes—or clubs, in this case—and I do not come in person to pick up mending, but it was urgently requested that I come, so here I am."

She was a very slim woman, with skinny limbs and a frowning face. Her energy reminded Art of industrious little birds that constantly scolded their young.

"My thanks for coming," Art said. The maid discreetly left and shut the door behind her as Charlotte picked up the mangled bustle.

"What happened to this?" she said. "It looks like you fell on it!"

"I did," Art said. "Many times. Did thee design it?"

"Yes," Charlotte said. She picked up the corset and her

fingers poked through one of the bitten-out holes. "And the corset. I've patented them."

"I am deeply thankful for thy corset's superior flexibility," Art said. "It served well during time of action. I've need of the same freedom in my bodice."

"You mean—oh, I see what you mean," Charlotte said when she picked up the bodice. The seams at the shoulders had burst again. "You're a very active woman."

"'Tis the work," Art said. Charlotte dropped the bodice and studied Art critically.

"They were cut to your measurements as given me by the Secret Commission, but your arms are. . . unlike the norm for our sex. And the breadth of you. I'll need to measure you myself."

"Please," Art said.

Charlotte pulled out her measuring tape from her carpet bag and set to work.

"I've brought my book," Charlotte said while she had Art raise her arms. "Will you look and then choose?"

"I will, but what thee designed suited best. No ribbons or bows. No heavy skirts, for I need my feet for running. No stripes or printed patterns. And. . . " Art decided to be brave and say it. "No bustle."

"I understand," Charlotte said. "You need street apparel, and yet must keep company with the better classes. I've a design in mind. It should be ready by midday, tomorrow."

"Thy speed impresses, but I don't want thy seamstresses overworked," Art said.

"My shop is supplied with sewing machines," Charlotte said. "Well lit, well aired, and the women know to eat. What work I do send out I make sure that woman is trained and given a machine as well. Whoever stays at the shop to finish wants to be there and is paid accordingly. No need to worry," she added in a curt tone.

"My admiration, Friend," Art said.

Charlotte wrapped the tape around Art's hips. "Word has already spread about the boy and Madame Beauchamp," Charlotte muttered. "Can't say I blame the mother though, despite the unfortunate result. Poor wretch."

"Thee has children?" Art asked.

"Yes, two." Charlotte's face softened.

"If thee should lose one as that seamstress had, and the police had the body. . . what would thee do?"

"Had the—what a horrible question! I don't care if they'd need to examine, I'd go down to their mortuary and claim my child right away!" Charlotte exclaimed.

Art quickly moved for the bed. She picked up her stockings, and though they had holes she pulled them on.

"Wait, what's happened?" Charlotte said. She went to Art and began helping her dress.

"The deaths are not done," Art simply said. While Charlotte swiftly applied the button hook to Art's boots Art slipped on the torn chemise and picked up the corset; someone had attempted to fix the pulled-out boning and it was bent back in again. Charlotte helped to lace the corset and tie it.

"This dress is a fright," Charlotte said once Art was in her torn under-bodice and under skirt. Charlotte held up the ragged skirt. "Don't end up dead again, or else the police will examine the labels and everyone will know I let you out dressed like this."

"I promise. I will take better care of thy designs," Art said. Soon she was fully dressed, though her sleeves were ripped and the bodice and skirt shredded.

"You look like a costumed actress from a tragedy. Sit. I can arrange your hair." Charlotte moved adeptly with the brush and pins. She swept Art's hair into an attractive bun. "A long time ago I was a lady's maid," she said. She retrieved Art's hat. "This still looks good, but I'll be ordering two more for you. And several pairs of gloves. And stockings. You'll need handkerchiefs."

Art rose and retrieved her stick. She picked up her keys. "My thanks, Friend. Now I must go."

She left Charlotte in her room and passed through the doors in ghost form. Out in the hall she saw the Russian, Oleg, standing stoically before a set of doors.

"Is my Friend Jim within?" Art asked him.

Oleg merely raised a fist and knocked on the door.

"Go away!" Jim cried from inside.

Oleg repeated his knock.

"I said, go away!" Jim shouted.

Art took ghost form. Oleg moved aside in alarm as Art poked her head inside.

"Friend, I must speak with thee," Art said. Jim was seated in a chair before a large bed, smoking a cigar. He hopped around in surprise at Art's voice. Then Art saw Arlette and Manon. They were both naked, Arlette on top and Manon lying beneath her.

Manon turned her head and her green eyes, large and deep, caught Art's and held her fast.

"Art, what's the matter? What's happened?" Jim asked.

"Forests," Art said.

"What? Art, as you Quakers say, plain words!" Jim demanded. Art shook herself from Manon's gaze.

"Friend, if I were the re-animationist I might make plans to not remain dead," Art said to him.

Jim's cigar fell from his teeth. "Don't just stand there in the hall looking in, come get me! I can guess which mortuary they took him to because of where he died. Let's go!"

Art ghosted in and looked to the bed apologetically. Arlette's face was mirthful. Manon's had softened, but her unwavering eyes still pulled Art in. Art grabbed Jim and hastily made an apology to the women. She exited quickly.

"They didn't mend your clothes!" Jim said as she ran them down the stairs to the main floor. "No matter, my stalwart strongwoman! To the street! We'll strike fear in the hearts of evil with your pale yet impressive muscles!"

"Thee calls me strong, yet I've met many stronger women today," she said dolefully as the footwoman hastily activated the iris door.

Jim laughed.

CHAPTER SIX

Shoreditch Mortuary was only a mile away. Art chose to run through the nighttime streets rather than take the hansom cab Jim suggested. Her glowing body lit the darkness between the gaslights, and her ragged skirts flapped. They arrived at the churchyard cemetery that lay beside the mortuary just as the bells tolled the hour. Beyond the mortuary was the undertaker's darkened cottage. A church loomed in the distance.

"Nice haunt," Jim said. "Let's read its aura."

Art stood still by the cemetery's wrought iron fence and felt none of the eldritch blackness she'd become familiar with. Yet she sensed, rolling softly like the white fog that covered the grounds of the churchyard, a spreading spell that nearly made her somnambulate. Oddly, she could taste its woven parts: earth, wind, and wood.

"That doesn't feel very high magic," Jim muttered.

"'Tis earth," Art said in surprise.

"Yes. Very ancient, that. Let's sneak through the back."

Art tossed Jim over the fence while she passed through in ghost form. As she negotiated the uneven cemetery ground beneath the fog, she recalled when she last felt an 'earth' quality from another.

"Friend," Art asked in a low voice. "If I might ask. Manon is—"

"A very beautiful girl, isn't she?" Jim interrupted softly. "Very popular with the painters."

"Aye," Art whispered. "Yet I felt—"

"That she prefers to stay at the Vesta and be a woman-in-residence? Yes, she does."

Art looked at Jim.

"You know, Art," Jim said. "Though we are extraordinary creatures as brought back with magic and science, the supernatural is not the mere handiwork of men—despite what men think. Dryads and nymphs. Sirens and centaurs and. . . imps. Real ghosts and real dragons. I bet they're around. But I also bet they don't let us see them unless they really want us to. Aren't we lucky when they do?"

"Aye," Art said thoughtfully. "We are."

"Door's ajar, Art," Jim whispered.

Art tripped over something. She glanced down. She felt about the ground fog. She pulled up a policeman by the front of his uniform.

"Dead?" Jim asked.

"Asleep," Art said. "Very." She laid the man carefully back down.

They approached the darkened building's back porch and its open door. Art went to the shuttered windows and poked her head through as a ghost. Inside was the viewing room with its glass coffins. Inspector Risk and several of his men were present, deeply asleep where they sat or fell. Art removed her head to let Jim know.

"Looks like Risk had the same thought as you!" Jim whispered. "He should have had us join him."

"We might have ended up the same," Art whispered back. "Dost thee suspect the re-animationist is still here?"

They heard the muffled sound of a woman's voice, deep

within the mortuary. She was wailing.

"I think that's our answer," Jim whispered.

"Shall I enter and we try the monocles?" Art asked.

"Two pairs of eyes in the room would be better," Jim said. "I'm not easily bewitched. Not sure why, perhaps because I'm mere bone and empty of organic matter. If our man's risen, be prepared for a battle. But the one mourning may be our real re-animationist."

Art hefted her stick and entered.

She passed the glass coffins, one of which held a dead child, stepped into a lab room, and then into a chamber containing a gas powered disinfecting oven. The woman's cries grew louder. Art entered the mortuary's dead room.

Before her were the cold slabs that held the dead. Farthest from her was a slab where the dead re-animationist was laid, a white sheet drawn down to his waist. Chance was caressing his face and weeping. She wore a black veil. In her hand she held a gnarled staff of pale wood and Art came to a halt at the sight of it. The wood emanated power.

Art moved silently forward. The closer she approached, the more the staff's energy brightened to her senses like the presence of sun and life.

Chance looked up and transfixed Art with a powerful stare. A silent command entered Art's mind, one that caused her to fall still. She could no longer move.

A *stupor*, Art thought. But she did not become insensate; she remained aware and standing.

"You killed my son," Chance accused, her words raw.

"I must disagree," Jim said. "He made his choice, jumping between buildings. Why didn't he just give himself up?"

"Why don't we ask him when he rises again?" Chance said. She sobbed and held the dead man to her.

"Madame, is that what you want?" Jim said gently. "You said so yourself, it won't be him. A woman like you, who counsels grieving women and understands the reality of soul and body? Yet you taught your boy reanimation."

"I didn't teach him," Chance retorted angrily. "He sought the knowledge himself. It obsessed him. Revenge twisted him," she whispered. "But it worked. My murdered granddaughter rose and obeyed my son's summons to the letter. Clara did what the police could not. Only she knew who her killer was and ran to him and killed him. She gave her father his vengeance."

"But it wasn't enough. Your son couldn't stop with Clara," Jim said.

"I wish he had," Chance cried. "Even when I found out about the others I couldn't stop him! He'd come to mortuaries like this one and look at the bodies of street urchins. He picked who died from violation, from violence. He raised them. And then he came to me. 'Mother,' he said. 'You summon for the grieved every day. You know which child died wrongly. You know we can help them.' I gave in the day I summoned a little girl who knew she wasn't the sole victim of her murderer. What if that murderer killed again? The police would never believe me, just like with Clara! Especially when the killer was respectable!" she spat.

"Yet now the decision is yours alone," Jim said. "Yours, Madame. For your own son, whose troubled heart is finally at peace."

Chance laughed bitterly. "He made me promise," she said.

"And as his mother, you already know in your own heart what's best," Jim said. "To leave him be."

Chance pointed the staff at Jim.

"Hypocrite," she said. "I've seen you. The things you've done, the sanctity of time's laws that you broke, all for your own selfishness! We are mortal for a reason, and yet you still worked to make certain she would never know rest! Thank your 'Friend,'" Chance cried, turning to Art. "Thank your foolish, meddling friend! For how did he absolve himself of the knowledge?

By not even remembering why he wanted it in the first place!"

"Wacko," Jim said in frustration. "All right, then." He began to glow in Art's hand. Heat seared her palm. A fire abruptly flared around him.

The pain roused Art from her paralysis. She rushed towards Chance. The woman flung the white staff to Art who caught it. Chance opened her arms wide.

"Come!" she cried to Art. "I am your first sacrifice, Dark Victorian!"

When Art neared, Chance grabbed Jim from Art's hand and held him close. His flame exploded in wild tendrils that spread over her entire body. Jim tumbled from her arms and bounced upon the mortuary floor, his flame gone.

"HELL!" Jim cried. "Oh God and HELL!"

Chance fell upon her son and the flames swiftly spread to swallow him up. Above the roar of the fire Art heard Risk.

"Men!" Risk shouted from the back of the mortuary. "Wake up! I think there's a fire!"

Art picked Jim and his smoldering hat up. She exited from the rapidly smoking room just as hurrying policemen entered from the other end. Once in the mortuary's reception area, Art climbed out of the nearest window and shut it behind her.

"I can't leave yet, Art, I. . . " Jim said helplessly.

Art threw her stick and the staff up on the mortuary roof. She climbed up and placed them near the chimney of the reception room. They sat, listening to the police shout and procure water for the flames. One policeman had the presence of mind to open windows, and the smell of burning flesh filled the air.

"Damn it," Jim finally whispered as they heard water splashing below. "Why did she. . . ? Damn it all."

"'Twas suicide," Art softly said. "She snatched thee, and I felt that she controlled the spread of thy flame. 'Twas unnatural. She passed it to her son deliberately."

"I didn't suspect it. Not at all," Jim said. "She didn't seem the sort. And yet. . . she can see the future, or what she thinks is one. Did she see this?"

"We will always guess," Art said. "But truth; she's made certain her son and herself will never rise again."

⤬

Once Jim was reassured that Risk had the fire in hand, Art left the mortuary roof and silently slipped away into the night's darkness. She had run them half a mile back to the Vesta before Jim spoke again.

"Thank you for protecting me, Art," he said, as Art slowed on the road to hear him. "It was wise what you did. The affair would have only gotten messier had we stayed. Your quick thinking also saved us from giving up her staff. It's something the police ought not to have."

"Friend, had it been just myself I would have remained," Art said. "Yet my heart said with the police there, thee should be taken away and quickly. 'Tis an act I might ponder later, though I doubt it needed." She lifted Chance's staff. "'Tis a remarkable wood," she said in awe. The staff felt like life was present in her hand.

"Art! What of your poor hand? I'm sorry I burned it," Jim said, contrite.

"'Tis healed, Friend. The staff did it."

"It did?" Jim said. "But of course it did. It's so. . . well, I haven't words for how that staff feels. Such a contrast from the son's unholy power. That poor fool."

Art placed her stick on the arm that held Jim up and raised the staff so he could admire it too. She thought it pure and perfect and she had the irrational desire to eat of it.

"Amazing, isn't it?" Jim said in a hushed voice.

"I want it inside me," Art said.

"Whaaat?" Jim said.

"Aye. Dost thee not want it inside thineself?" Art asked.

"Good God, woman, would you—all right, put me on top, I'm exhausted from that stupid fire trick. I need smokes, but I'm too sad to eat. I'm sure this stick will feel amazing."

Art placed Jim atop the head of the staff and held him aloft like a severed head upon a pike. Jim began to glow softly, a warm yellow aura. A hansom cab entered the road Art walked down, but upon seeing them the driver hastily brought his horses around again.

"Oh, I'm a godling," Jim said peacefully.

"Be not above thy Light," Art said.

"You were the one who wanted it inside you. Art, when Chance talked of her grandchild a realisation came to me, one that has caused unattended pieces to fall into place. We've one more task. The night, unfortunately, remains young. How about it my young friend, you up to it?"

"We are spectres. Ours is the night," Art said.

"Then take us back to Bloomsbury."

∾

They spent the hours after midnight in the peaceful darkness of a row of neat and ordered houses. Art and Jim sat at the Hillings kitchen porch beneath their lemon tree. Unlike inner London, not one cab or cart could be heard. When a lone horse and cart graced the street, Art and Jim watched them pass, both animal and driver oblivious to the slight glow Art gave from the porch. The two whiled the time away in thought or in casual conversation of things that came to mind.

"British Museum's just over there. If you haven't visited before your death, we ought to check out the Grecian marbles. I know you'll enjoy those. And the Egyptian antiquities. I like the mummies," Jim said.

'*Check out,*' Art thought. It was another of Jim's queer phrases, but it made sense.

"We've an object even older and rarer in our hands," Art said, admiring the staff again. "Yet we must relinquish it."

"Relinquish? No, we keep it, and better yet, we hide it," Jim said. "Even if it means sending the precious thing away."

Art looked at Jim.

"I've learned never to let such objects—or persons—end up in Fall's hands," Jim said. "He's not the only one in that building who'll break something apart just to see how it ticks. And sometimes what they take apart is alive. Trust me on this, Art."

"Very well, Friend," Art said pensively. "As thee had said. . . about dryads, centaurs, and dragons."

"And imps," Jim soberly added. "I wonder if Chance had a bit of creature in her? She looked more the wife of her own son than the mother."

"Her youth may be attributed to this," Art said, indicating the staff. "She'd a piece of the Tree of Life."

"Art!" Jim laughed. "The Tree is not real, it's an allegory! One of those maps of magical systems. Hence the high magic. There is no such tree existing."

"If thee says so," Art said, smiling.

They fell silent. The night sky's furthest edge became touched with light. Blue began to appear.

"What did she mean, naming me "Dark Victorian"?" Art mused.

"Odd thing to say," Jim said. "We're typical of Her Majesty, for it is our Queen's time. It's like saying you're dark furniture or dark curtains. Or a dark china pattern."

"I regret not carrying pen and paper. I shall forget her words," Art said.

"I haven't the faintest idea what she was ranting about that was supposedly about me," Jim muttered.

Art recalled how Chance stared at her while accusing Jim of unknown acts. Strong foreboding words, yet because of the mystery of them Art was ambivalent about taking Chance's warnings to heart.

"'Twill be or not be," Art simply said.

"Art, please," Jim said in a suffering voice. "No Hamlet." He sighed. "It's just as well. What if you knew your grandchild would die violently, that your son will turn to dark works and be consumed by them, or that you might resign yourself in the end to flames? If I knew these things or had it told to me in riddles, I'd want it all excised from my mind. I prefer chance and free will. Especially while enjoying our second chance at life. Good God, I wonder if her name was bitter humour on her part."

"Her naming was apt," Art said. "All have the Light of God. We learn and we choose, and we may choose unwisely. We know not if she saw past or future. Anything may change; this was the message of her name."

"I forgot that you Quakers don't believe in predestination," Jim said mischievously. "If the official religion hears I must prevent your burning."

"Let them try," Art said.

The door opened behind them and Mary gave a muffled shriek. Jim twisted around upon the step.

"Mary! It's just us, sorry to have surprised you!" Jim said. "We're here on business, as per usual for us agents. How are you? And is it breakfast time already?"

⤨

The smell of cooking filled the kitchen. Jim sat on a fine napkin at the Hillings' dining table amid toast, butter, jam, poached eggs, broiled fish, a slice of ham, and blood sausage. Mary entered and laid down a small plate of bacon. In her nervousness she reset the marmalade jar to another spot on the table.

"They're here, sir," she whispered loudly to Jim. "They won't eat anythin', though."

"Wrap them a sandwich to take with, Mary," Jim suggested in a low voice. She nodded and left.

"Hello, my Cheshire Cat, where art thou?" Jim whispered.

Art materialised in ghost form, standing at the opposite end of the table. She smiled at him. They'd just discovered that when she fully ghosted away she became invisible. She solidified in order to reach over and straighten Jim's top hat.

"My Mad Hat must look a sight," Jim said, realising he still smelt burnt.

They heard Mr. Hillings descend the staircase and Art slowly disappeared. Mr. Hillings entered. His bored gaze was cool. A white bandage was taped over his throat, but his movements were little affected by his recent injury. He sat down to his breakfast, retrieved his paper, then paused to sniff the air curiously.

"Good morning, Mr. Hillings, I'm Jim Dastard," Jim said.

Mr. Hillings jumped and lost all color at the sight of Jim at his table. He clutched his newspaper to his breast.

"We hadn't met earlier due to your being in a faint," Jim said. "I'm from the Secret Commission and have been investigating your wife and baby's murder. We're very sorry for your loss, sir."

"S-Secret Commission," Mr. Hillings said. He tried to relax. "I understand."

"It was your three-year-old child, recently deceased, who attacked you?" Jim asked.

"It was, sir. I gave that information to the police at hospital," Mr. Hillings said.

"I've come to let you know that you needn't fear her returning again," Jim said. "Your revenant daughter has been destroyed."

Mr. Hillings gave a deep sigh of relief. "Thank God," he said. "That. . . abomination. My wife should have never—but it's all done now."

"It almost is," Jim said. "We've only to arrest little Ella's killer now."

Mr. Hillings slowly put his paper down.

"Mr. Hillings, you had three daughters before Ella, all dead from illness?" Jim said. "What cruel and horrible luck. Yet we know you tried your best, insisting on the latest pharmaceutical medicines and prayer. So maddening to have incompetent doctors examine your daughters and not diagnose adequate relief or cure! No wonder you finally refused their expertise. Your wife gave Ella her medicines religiously. Mary says that every day, on the hour, Mrs. Hillings fed Ella her doses, praying for recovery. Strange that we can no longer find the bottles."

"So why did you kill your daughters, Mr. Hillings?" Jim said. "Why poison them? The re-animationist answered that question. Ella was raised from death for a single purpose: vengeance. She killed the mother who unknowingly poisoned her, and she killed the baby brother who was to take her place: the true Hillings heir, a handsome boy and not the waste of money and breath those troublesome daughters would have been. But wait; that pride and joy of your loins is DEAD too, isn't he?"

Mr. Hillings rose and grabbed the silver tray from the side console. He raised it above his head to bring it down on Jim. Art solidified and grabbed Mr. Hillings' by the nape of the neck. She pulled him back as his arms came down with the tray, hitting nothing. She took the tray from him.

"My wife was the one who killed the little brat!" Mr. Hillings sputtered. "Once I remarry I'll have another son!"

"Oh, I doubt that, because you won't have a chance to fornicate before being hanged," Jim coldly said. Two plainclothes policemen grimly entered the dining room from the kitchen. Art gave Mr. Hillings to them. As they exited, Jim stared at the cooling breakfast on the table.

"Stupid waste," he said.

⤳

When Art stepped out the back porch of the Hillings home, Mary was seated at the kitchen table with the paper, glumly looking for open positions. The policemen marched their prisoner to their cab and left. The morning sky brightened and birds sang. A man came with fresh buns loaded on a tray and made a delivery.

"Nice of Mary to feed you the uncooked herring, but it makes you smell a bit fishy, Art," Jim complained.

"Mary," Art said. "Thee has mint at the window. May I have some?"

"Please, Miss, as much as you want," Mary said mournfully. "There'll be no one here to tend them, soon."

Art absorbed a handful of sprigs while Jim bade Mary farewell.

Art took them from the sedate environs of Bloomsbury to visit Fiona Bell, the widow of the slaughterman, who lived near Whitechapel Market. Jim's spirits picked up once back in the bustle of the East End. When she finally walked them back to the Vesta, Inspector Risk was stepping out of a cab. He waved to them.

"Ar! My burnt hat and you smelling of fire as well," Jim said. "Time to come clean. You go ahead on up. We'll have a man-to-man talk, he and I."

"I've no need to worry?" Art asked as she neared Risk, who appeared to be in a good mood.

"No," Jim said. "He just wants to update me on the case. And I should tell him about the Hillings arrest if he hasn't been told already. We've an understanding, and no matter what I share, he and his men still look good at the close of this."

Art gave Jim to Inspector Risk once they greeted each other and let them into the Vesta with her key. Doris showed Risk and Jim a waiting room where they could speak privately. Art moved for the stairs. Two men in the curiousities and mechanical room, one with his arm fondly around the other, were enjoying how the morning light lit the stereoscope cards they were viewing. Men and women seated in the facing drawing rooms brought their papers down to watch Art pass. Alice bade her a good morning as Art ascended the staircase, her ragged skirt trailing.

Art saw Oleg seated and reading a paper in the hall. She walked to her room and retrieved her room key from her dress pocket. She beheld it in bemusement, realising then that she was a woman with a place and possessions.

A door opened down the hall. Manon, disheveled and wearing only a dressing gown, stared at Art with wide eyes. Her gaze went to the staff in Art's hand. She ran barefoot down the hall just as Art unlocked her door to enter. Manon's gown fluttered open. Disconcerted, Art entered her room and Manon followed her.

Art stood in the center of her bedroom with her stick and Chance's staff clutched to her. Manon stopped and stared. Oleg appeared behind, watching curiously through the open door. Manon appeared ready to leap.

Art quickly held the staff out to her.

Wonder grew upon Manon's face and then pure joy. She made a sound, but it manifested as the rush of wind upon Art, exuberant with the sweeping undulation of branches and leaves. Art felt long grass wave through her. The sensation swept her off her feet; the next thing she saw was the decorative moulding of the ceiling.

Manon instantly appeared above, her light weight atop Art. She held the staff against her joyful face. She kissed the wood.

"Will thee hide it?" Art asked. She was surprised she could still think. Manon simply smiled. She held Art's face and gently kissed her, her blonde hair tickling. She slid off. Art heard the swift patter of Manon's feet and she and Oleg were gone.

"Art, what happened? Seen a mouse and fainted?" Jim said from the doorway. Art struggled to sit. Alice was holding Jim and she entered. With her face politely composed, she set Jim and a folded newspaper upon the table by the brightly lit window. The drawn curtains filled the room with sun. Once Alice left, Art stood up. She straightened her hat.

"There are better ways to enjoy the sight of the ceiling," Jim said.

"I am realising it, Friend," Art said.

"Well, Risk knows now how things went at the mortuary," Jim said. "If I'd a nose I'd be tapping the side of it. Time to celebrate! But it's only late morning, therefore the girls will be asleep," he added sadly. "Bless their beautiful, hardworking bodies. Art, look there, you've gained a modest trousseau!"

Since Jim could not point, Art turned in the direction of his line of vision. The sunlight fell on her closet. The armoire was ajar, displaying a new dress hung upon the door and hat boxes lined on the top shelf. Recalling Charlotte's words, Art thought she might find new stockings, undergarments, and handker-chiefs in the dresser drawers. She stepped forward and her stick hit something. She looked down. Embedded in the carpet was a child's tooth.

"More and more, you're becoming a real lady," Jim said with admiration as Art picked up the tooth. She slowly moved for the dresser. She placed the tooth on it and removed her hat and gloves. "Soon you'll pick a surname. Start banking your money. Why, later if you want to debut as an eligible bachelorette among all those toms, I may have to chaperone you. But first we have to get you out of your ragged clothes. You also need reminding of how to properly relax and let go of your stick."

Art observed her hand. Jim was correct; she still held her walking stick. She didn't feel like putting it down just yet.

"I'll remember, Friend," Art said. She found a large white box in the armoire and placed it on the bed. She opened it. Inside was a rolled corset, newly built, with the shaped plates between the boning that were Charlotte's design.

Art remembered the bent bone of her damaged corset and touched her side. Her fingers entered the tear in her bodice and undergarments. She realised the bone had protected her rib.

"Art, your idea of relaxation is visiting a mourning widow," Jim said. "Though she was a pretty Irish lass. I'm glad it wasn't shopping, but will you next convince me to visit a Midnight Mission?"

"Thee said thee would tolerate me in my support of widows," Art said.

"Orphaned widows! And Mrs. Bell was clearly not orphaned, as her mother was present and alive enough to give you a piece of her mind. I'm surprised she had any to spare."

"'Tis her right. I did kill Fiona's husband," Art said quietly. She covered the corset box.

"And unlike some, you care, and returned to help. Well, I understand the wife's lingering anger. Her children have taken to you though, and they know about their father," Jim said.

"The boy and little girl are sweet," Art said smiling briefly. "She—" Art suddenly stopped speaking.

"Art?" Jim asked. Art pressed a hand to her mouth.

"Art. . . " Jim said when her fingers began to shake.

"I—hit the littlest one," Art said. "I—smashed her, I," she convulsed. "I smashed them all—I couldn't let them leave—"

She sobbed. She fell to her knees. Her cries grew jagged and wild. Art curled on the floor. In agony she wailed.

Jim watched the sun's rays move down the walls and shorten. He listened until Art's sobs quieted into tearful breathing. When she had calmed and he thought she might even be asleep, he spoke.

"I believe," he said softly to her. "That wherever they are, they forgive you."

Afternoon in London; the haze of the smoke-filled sky took on a different cast and shadows grew in mark of the time. Clerks emerged from their buildings to catch transportation back to their towns and homes while workmen trudged with their meal cans and tools to their nighttime jobs. A woman walked solemnly among them in a high-collared long black coat. She held a black book to her breast. She wore no hat or gloves. Helene Skycourt bought a paper from a towheaded boy hawking the latest news about the rogue re-animations. She continued alongside the trundling carts and carriages until she came upon a small street where a crowd of people gathered. They were staring at the decrepit tenement building, no longer deserted, where all the reanimated child corpses had met their end. Several poor families were moving their possessions up the steps. One costermonger sold boiled whelks nearby. Ragged boys surrounded one spot on the walk with glee, gesturing and talking about the event amongst themselves. When Helene spied over their heads, she saw the dried smear of black blood on the stone.

"She's seven feet tall, I heard, a giant!" one boy exclaimed.

"And she carries a stick, like a cudgel! With spikes! Crush! You're dead!" another laughed, demonstrating with his own arms.

"Is it the Blackheart?" the youngest urchin asked.

"No, it's a Secret Policeman," an elder boy said. He clenched a clay pipe between his teeth.

Helene moved away and walked down the street, leaving the loitering crowd behind. A short distance away she found a man selling fried eels. After a few words, she paid him the amount Helia owed him. Then she walked home.

Helene was about to mount the steps into her tenement building when she spotted Helia weaving her penny-farthing frantically through the traffic. Once she reached Helene, Helia hopped off her wheel. She also had a paper under her arm. She looked at Helene and paused.

"You've met," Helia said. "Already."

"She's alive," Helene merely said. She turned. The steps in

her building also led down to a basement meeting room. Upon the closed door below was a sign: The Society of Friends.

Helene climbed the steps for the floor above the Friends' meeting place. Her door, unlike the other apartment doors, was thick and faced with a large brass panel. It had a tiny label plate that read: THUNDERBOLT DOOR. PAT. NO 116636-14. DEC.1876, SKYCOURT INDUSTRIES, LONDON, ENGLAND. Helene slid the panel open. She quickly typed a combination on the lettered keys. If she typed it wrong, the panel would shut on her hand. The door opened, and Helia followed her sister in.

Inside her apartment Helene removed her spectacles and unfolded her paper. Her quarters held a simple bed, black stove, a desk, and one shelf with books. The place lacked wallpaper and decoration, but pinned on one wall in an ordered pattern of gathered research were news clippings, maps, and notes. At her desk was a stack of business papers bearing the stationary head of Skycourt. Her black travel case lay atop. She sat on the sill and read by the light of the window while Helia cleared books from a chair. Helia found the note she'd scrawled to her sister recently and stuck in Helene's door panel. She read it.

When will you give all this up? Helia had written. Helene had written in answer beneath:

When you give up living in a balloon.

Helia briefly laughed, then sat down and pulled out her cigarette case and match safe from a pocket. She lit a cigarette. She smoked and rocked.

"Did you greet her?" she asked.

"Not so much that," Helene murmured.

"I was busy. Very busy, else I'd told you sooner. The Secret Commission only released her, oh, more than a day ago? She and her partner solved the case just this morning. Back to Bloomsbury I rode, before the maid vacated. And I had that and the other story needing following. I barely made the afternoon press."

"I'm reading it," Helene said.

"You can lay this one to rest now. I wondered why you couldn't discover the reanimations first. And take care of it."

"I discovered them, but wards were used, misdirecting me," Helene muttered as she read. "However, the re-animationist was weakening. I might have gotten to him. And to them." She turned a page of the newspaper. "You've written about her. You've made her a hero."

"Jealous?" Helia said. She laughed, but her humour faded as quickly as it came. Her eyes grew stark as she smoked.

"Even before, she was my hero," she whispered. "Handling the worse in me. And yet I did it to her again. I saw her when she'd come out after killing those creatures. Her eyes, her eyes, her eyes. . . " Helia's own eyes closed. "I've hurt her all over again."

"She was Quaker, Helia, what did you expect?" Helene said sharply. "This is why I was against it, she should have been left to rest!"

"You're wrong!" Helia snapped. "If you really saw her, saw her as I did when she first set foot out of the Secret Commission! You'd accept that Art deserves life again!"

Helene stared at her sister, her mouth a thin line.

"You'll. . . you'll get used to it," Helia chuckled. She resumed smoking. "Especially when the bills come in. I'm paying for her clothes. Well, you're paying for her clothes. Lottie will have a bill for you."

"Helia," Helene said. "That's not how she—"

"No," Helia said. "This time—how do those Quakers say it? She's to have it worldly! I even gave Art one of your stick designs, and she's taken so well to it, you should see!" She pointed at her sister. "And you agreed; this is our chance to support her as we failed to do before. I'm well and truly a pauper now. I've signed over my latest *Times* check to that hideous Fall.

But that's the last payment he'll demand from me for resurrecting Art. It was probably a ruse to get me to visit. He's so curious about this." She motioned to the masked side of her face. "The way his lenses kept clicking, trying to SEE it." She snickered. "Thinks he can get at it. Doesn't know that it would get him." Her eyes sparkled with mirth.

Helene stared at the masked side of her sister's face, remembering a time when Helia didn't wear the leather. Even then Helia had tried to tell her something was there, though all Helene saw were the scars. Her sister's words had always been riddles, mad sayings. It had seemed best back then to send Helia away to doctors and asylums.

"It won't let me tell you!" Helia would cry, laughing like a madwoman.

Art was the one who somehow understood, yet even when Art told her Helene was slow to believe.

"Your. . . it's been dormant a while now," Helene said cautiously.

"Oh, that's because Art makes it so," Helia said. "When I'm in love I'm not, well, you know. Trying to have people kill me." She chuckled again. "I tried so hard with you. Called you names and everything. Then, one shot!" Helia cocked a hand at the masked side of her face. "It would be gone!"

"Hush," Helene said. She took a breath. "I'd never, ever seriously wanted to hurt you."

"There's time yet," Helia said. "But now. . . Art's here again." She seemed to bask in the knowledge.

Helene's face grew stern. She returned her attention to the paper.

"I looked in on her, Helene," Helia said. "Had to after all the killing. I think she'll be all right. Yes, right. Right, right, right. Right as rain." Helia laughed. "She might be the first to survive me. Isn't that funny?"

"Well, she is one of them now, isn't she?" Helene coolly said.

"One of those creatures."

Helia closed her eyes. "She's magnificent."

Wisps of smoke rose from her cigarette as Helia fell into recall. Helene stared at her paper, her mind's eye bleakly remembering another Art.

"And like any magnificent creature she attracts other creatures," Helia added, stirring. Her face brightened. "She's staying at the Vesta."

Helene lowered her paper.

"Oh, don't give me that look! It's entirely respectable, or else you wouldn't have a membership! Though they've long revoked mine."

"When you said you looked in, you mean—" Helene said.

"Yes," Helia interrupted. "Exactly. The cook let me in. And then I found out that Art fancied one of the French girls. The one like that novel. Mano—"

Helia stood up, upsetting the chair. Her hands went to the masked side of her face, the cigarette between her fingers nearly stabbing her eye.

"Oh you don't LIKE her do you, and I know why, because Manon is the oppos—I—you—I'll kill you—look—LOOK," Helia ground out. Her hands clutched at her face as if holding something.

Helene quickly donned her spectacles. The bewitched lenses revealed the eldritch infection that lived in the left side of Helia's face; its shadowy, tendriled web crawled in her sister's flesh. It slithered. Helene recalled Art's words from long ago.

"'Tis venom," Art's voice said in Helene's mind. "And it fears its own death."

Helene leapt forward and grabbed Helia's arms before her hands could tear at it. She removed the cigarette. She shushed her sister and made soothing noises.

"I saw it," Helene reassured. "I saw it better this time. Let it go." She picked up the fallen chair and made Helia sit in it.

The virus in Helia's face writhed.

"Since you're listening to me, LISTEN—" Helia cried.

"Yes, what is it? Tell me," Helene urged.

"It knows death," Helia said. "It can always see it. By equal turn, it knows LIFE when it sees it. Helene." Helia clutched her sister. "Manon is that. Don't ask me what that might be. If Art wants her, you will pay for it."

Helene's jaw dropped.

"We can pretend Manon's your Convenient, if you're worried about Art's respectability," Helia suggested. She gasped and laughed. "You and Malcom were lovers for years and he was married. And yes, everyone knew. Your reputation can survive keeping a prostitute."

"Now you jest with me!" Helene said. "You say you love Art, but—"

"Whatever she may want," Helia said firmly. "Anything. Because it's our second chance. You said you'd listen."

"Yes, but I didn't say I'd agree, or understand!" Helene cried. Despite her own confusion, Helene could see with her lenses that her sister had recovered. The masked side of Helia's face no longer crawled with the virus it harbored. It was smooth once more.

Helia giggled.

"Asleep again," she said. She smiled as she gently removed Helene's spectacles. "Helene! What of my latest story? Did you find anything new? Because what I have will appear in the morning unless I rush them something different tonight."

Helene stood slowly. Her sister was calm and happy again, as if they hadn't talked of death, living venom, and of offering Art French women.

"It still stands at four dead," Helene said. "And I've yet to discover what links them."

"Three men and one woman found without their organs and bones," Helia said in hushed recall. "All victims still fully clothed, no signs of incision. Their blood continued to slowly drain from their orifices. They could only be identified by what was in their pockets and no apparent link between the victims. All were members of the lower classes. Blame might be given to criminals selling bodies to the medical vivisectionists."

Helene grasped Helia hands and coaxed her to stand.

"You need to sleep," Helene said gently. "If anything new happens tonight I'll let you know." She led her sister to the bed and removed Helia's hat. She pulled off her gloves.

"I'm hungry," Helia said. "And I want none of your horrid porridge, Helene! Perhaps by now you've learned to not burn it, but it's still disgusting."

"I'll fetch you something."

"You leave, and I'll look beneath your bed and go through your weapons," Helia threatened. She snickered.

"No you won't, because I've locked them. Now tell me what you'd like," Helene said, smiling.

"Something warm. Warm and heavy and satisfying. A pie. Oh, I saw her eat. It was thrilling! Like the agent who ate coal except more beautiful."

Helia lay down with a flop and sighed. She closed her eyes.

"I must see how she is in the morning," she said.

***

Art stepped through the Vesta's iris portal and set her stick upon the walk. She wore Charlotte's newly designed outfit, bustle-less and flexible. The rows of mother of pearl buttons on her bodice flashed in the sunlight. Jim sat in her left hand wearing his spare top hat. As she moved down the street through the throng of people he chatted animatedly about a popular co-medic play he'd seen. Would she like to see it? Art respectfully declined. She half listened as he went on to describe the story, characters, and antics of the actors. The sadness left her eyes whenever Jim recalled something humorous to share.

"There! Buy me that paper, Art. We didn't get to read the morning one, but I bet this one has the arrest in it. Miss Skycourt's probably written great things about us. And if she hasn't, I'll write a scathing response to the editorials. Ha ha! I'd like to read it later at the coffee shop."

While Art purchased the paper from the newsboy Jim hopped in her hand.

"Lucky us, I spy some of your brethren. Now's your chance, Art."

Art straightened and saw the Quaker couple Jim referred to. She crossed the street to greet them. They stood stock-still at the sight of her, but didn't run away.

"My pardon," she said gently to the plainly dressed couple. "Thy help is needed. Where might I find a meeting of Friends?"

After a half hour of conversation Art walked the Quaker couple, who were smiling and at ease, to their omnibus stop and watched them board and leave. She then entered a coffee shop and while Jim smoked at the table, she opened the paper and read aloud to him. A beggar woman gratefully accepted their offer of a cup of coffee and a meat pie.

The shadows lengthened and the lamplighters appeared, diligently lighting the gas lamps of the street. Art left the coffee shop behind and strolled further into the darker narrower streets, avoiding the filth on the ground as steam slowly rose from leaking pipes. Jim insisted on a penny gaff and she finally agreed. As he guided her to a location, men stood in the street and stared at her openly, wondering if she were a prostitute. Others skulked in the dark, measuring her as a possible robbery mark. A policeman and his small, spectacled companion who held a notebook stopped to study them and then walked away.

Art found the lit noisy entrance of a small theatre with brightly colored posters and shouldered past the startled young costermen smoking their pipes. She lowered her head to enter. Within, the enthusiastic audience vigorously thumped the tables. On the street a bright oil lamp mounted on the front of a penny-farthing bobbed in the dark. Helia Skycourt rode swiftly past.

End.

Additional
Content

Jim Dastard's Bon Mots
RISEN'S Illustration Plates
A glimpse into Dark Victorian: BONES

JIM DASTARD'S BON MOTS

A nice shot in the arm," [1916] Jim said sarcastically.
"Billy, God bless that dimwit [1921], was a voracious coal eater."
"Ha ha! Road kill [1972]," Jim said.
"Any of this giving you a ring?" [1910]
"Oh whammy [1940]," Jim said in disorientation.
That's right, look forward! Jerk [1896]," Jim said.
"Nice digs [1893], too," Jim said.
"Not that pneumatic [1950] body of yours but your mind."
"Wacko [1970]," Jim sighed.
"We ought to check out [1921] the Greek marbles."
"Time to come clean [1904]."

She was broad of shoulder, small of waist, and with a generous chest so
well-fitted by her bodice Jim felt she might deflect bullets.

Her eyes were blue, and at the sight of Artifice her lips parted and her eyes grew wide with a strange, deep delight and profound awe.

"Art!" Jim yelled when she dropped her ax. Then he saw why.
A weaponless slaughter man approached and threw a fist for her face.

"We're comin'. Take us out," one said to Art excitedly. The angry brothel-keeper blocked the door.
"We've a contract! They signed it and can't break it! You take them and the police
will just return the bitches, they're my property!" Sal screeched.

ELIZABETH WATASIN

The DARK
VICTORIAN

BONES

❖

A Glimpse Into:

Dark Victorian: BONES

"I Am Made Of This"

Chapter One

A heavy fog rolled through London. Gaslights broke the dark as a hackney carriage drove down a deserted, cobbled street. Inside the carriage, Inspector Risk, a tall, dark-haired man with a thick moustache, sat and grimly regarded Dr. Speller, a bespectacled man with white mutton chop sideburns seated across from him. Dr. Speller moved his top hat around in his hands in excitement. The plainclothes sergeant, Barkley, took notes.

"It's Esther Stubbings, I'm sure of it," Dr. Speller said. "She is one of your victims."

"I've four bodies," Risk said. "Just skin and muscle. Full skeletons and organs entirely removed and no incisions made. Makes it hard to identify flattened faces. You're claiming that the organ almost sold to you tonight belonged to this Esther Stubbings, and therefore she's my victim."

"Well I've yet to identify the body, but the organ is unquestionably hers, Inspector, because I was the surgeon," Speller said. "Every woman's reproductive organs are   different. I mean in shape. I recognized my own work, sir; I was the one who removed her second ovary. And Esther was alive and well just last week. The only way someone could harvest her organs is if she were murdered."

"And since we've her female vitals she has been," Risk said. "So this organ stealer, knowing you were a women's physician and vivisectionist; he comes to you for a sale."

"I vivisected only to learn," Speller said. "But for the most part I now merely dissect organs purchased solely from the Royal Surgical Sciences Academy."

"Yes. The Academy. Who buys from men like the one you met tonight," Risk said. "Except this one knows to bring it directly to you. The dead woman I have is of the poor. We know it from her clothes. How can someone like that afford your services?"

"She can when she volunteers for the procedure," Speller said. "Like all members of the Academy I'm a man of science and medicine. Not only do I use the skills learned, I practice new techniques that have successfully corrected female ailments. Esther Stubbings was on her way to becoming a fully healthy woman. And none of it, thankfully, by use of supernatural nonsense, claiming healing through organ transference and such!"

"But that's exactly what I have, doctor," Risk said. "Black arts surgery. Unless you can explain how four people have no skulls, eyes, or brains in their intact heads unless it was all pulled out of their nostrils."

"Not to mention," Sergeant Barkley said. "How His Royal Highness can be here with us today if not for supernatural medicine. Been nineteen years since he nearly died! We've a bunch of nonsense to thank."

Risk sighed while Speller glowered. The carriage came to a halt outside a lit station house.

"You stay here," Risk said to Speller. "We'll move on to the mortuary shortly for you to identify the woman. And you," he said to Barkley. "Stop talking. Let's go."

When Risk stepped down from the carriage he saw a young woman in an azure coat briskly leave the station entrance.

Her brown hat was crooked and wisps of dark hair escaped. Her skirts were cut high enough for the ankles of her boots to show. She wore a fitted leather mask on one side of her face. Helia Sky-court smiled at Risk and waved. She grabbed the penny-farthing resting against the station wall, took a running jump into the side-saddle seat, and hit the treadle. The lantern in front of her wheel suddenly lit. She sped away into the dark and fog.

Risk watched her depart, incredulous.

"Damn journalist," he said. "Does she never sleep?" Barkley stifled a yawn. They entered the station building.

"Inspector," Barkley said in a low voice as they walked into the dimly lit room. A uniformed man was behind the desk. "This case . . . it being supernatural. When will the Secret Commission start helping?"

"When we ask for it," Risk said curtly. "And not before. What do you have?" he said to the policeman who rose to greet him.

"Sir," the policeman said. He led them down a narrow hall. "The fellow Dr. Speller had us arrest will be brought out of his cell shortly. He refuses to speak and has answered no questions. The doctor told us the man only spoke once during the negotiating of the price of the organ and his accent was German."

"Looks a foreigner, then?" Risk asked. He followed the policeman into a room with a desk and chairs. He took the seat behind the desk while Barkley went to stand near the small, barred window.

"No sir," the policeman answered. "Well dressed, clean-faced, trimmed hair, tidy, hands that haven't seen hard labor. I'm guessing he's of the medical profession."

"Organ stealers usually are," Risk said. "Especially those who work in mortuaries." They heard shuffling steps approach. Two policemen brought a shackled man into the room. He was a slim fellow, tight-lipped and with one, nervous eye. His other eye was removed, leaving a gaping, black socket. He did not bother to shut his eyelid. The men escorting him sat him in front of Risk.

"*Wie ist dein name?*" Risk said.

The man looked at him in surprise.

"The sooner you answer our questions," Risk said.."The sooner we catch who's doing these black arts surgeries. Because it isn't you, is it? So if you don't want the blame, give us someone else's name."

The man's posture became stiffer.

"That's four dead," Risk said staring into the man's one eye. "Is the gallows worth this surgeon? Give him up and you won't have to worry. Do your sentence and then get on with life, right?"

Risk watched the man; the prisoner seemed to grow even more frightened.

"Right," Risk said slowly. "Now who is he?"

A shot exploded, shattering the window behind the sergeant. Blood sprayed into Risk's face. The other men shouted and ran out the door. The prisoner sat slumped. Brain matter hung from the side of his forehead where the exiting bullet had shattered the skull.

Shouts and running came from outside the station. Risk didn't bother looking out the broken window, knowing that all he'd see would be darkness and fog. He grimly pulled out his handkerchief and slowly wiped his face. Barkley touched the prisoner to see if he was still alive.

"Shall I send a message to the Secret Commission?" Barkley asked.

Risk stared at the dead man who'd just brought him an internal affairs nightmare.

"Do it," Risk said.

Read more in
Elizabeth Watasin's
Dark Victorian: BONES

The Author would like to Thank:

Phatpuppy Creations
phatpuppyart.com

Cover model, Elizabeth Worth
www.modelmayhem.com/3122503

Cavalyn Galano
for Custom Wardrobe Creation
www.facebook.com/CavalynDesign

Nadya Rutman for Makeup/Hair
www.bynadya.com

and

Teresa Yeh Photography
www.teresayeh.com

KEEP
CALM
GHOST
AND
SKULL
ARE
HERE

About The Author

Elizabeth Watasin is the acclaimed author of the Gothic steampunk novel *The Dark Victorian: RISEN* and the creator/artist of the indie comics series *Charm School*. She has worked as an animation artist on thirteen Disney feature films, including *Beauty and the Beast, Aladdin, The Lion King,* and *The Princess and the Frog,* and has written for *Disney Adventures* magazine. She lives in Los Angeles with her black cat named Draw, busy bringing readers uncanny heroines in shilling shockers and adventuress tales.

Follow the news of her latest projects at A-Girl Studio.
www.a-girlstudio.com
amazon.com/author/elizabethwatasin
www.facebook.com/ElizabethWatasinX
twitter.com/ewatasin

Look for Elizabeth's third gothic tale in The Dark Victorian series:
EVERLIFE.

Made in the USA
Monee, IL
08 October 2021

79609929R00081